SALUTE TO SPRING

For Gayle

Salute to th
Womens struggle
for

Meridel Le Sueur

INTERNATIONAL PUBLISHERS
381 Park Avenue South NEW YORK, N. Y. 10016

Salute to Spring
BY MERIDEL LE SUEUR

Salute to Spring

MERIDEL LE SUEUR

International Publishers
New York

First published by
International Publishers Co., Inc., New York, 1940
This edition is published simultaneously by
International Publishers, New York and
Seven Seas Books, Berlin, 1977

Library of Congress Cataloging in Publication Data
Le Sueur, Meridel.
Salute to spring.
CONTENTS: Corn village. – No wine in his cart. – Fable
of a man and pigeons. – A hungry intellectual. [etc.]
I. Title.
PZ3.L56783Sal10 [PS3523.E79] 813'. 5'2   75-38588
ISBN 0-7178-0463-1 pbk.

CONTENTS

Corn Village

St. Paul, 1930
Like many Americans, I will never recover from my
sparse childhood in Kansas. The blackness, weight and
terror of childhood in mid-America strike deep into the
stem of life. Like desert flowers we learned to crouch
near the earth, fearful that we would die before the
rains, cunning, waiting the season of good growth. Those
who survived without psychic mutilation have a life
cunning, to keep the stem tight and spare, withholding
the deep blossom, letting it sour rather than bloom and
be blighted.

Looking for nourishment, we saw the dreary villages,
the frail wooden houses, the prairies ravished, everything impermanent as if it were not meant to last the
span of one man's life, a husk through which human life
poured, leaving nothing behind, not even memory, and
every man going a lonely way in a kind of void, all
shouting to each other and unheard, all frightfully alone
and solitary.

And fear, fear everywhere on the streets in the gray
winter of the land, and the curious death in the air, the
bright surface activity of the pioneer town and the curious
air dissipating powers of fear and hate.

The Middle West is all so familiar to me and yet it
is always unfamiliar, a dream, an unreality. There are
Kansas, Iowa, Illinois, Nebraska. They were for a long
time frontier states. There villages are yet the waste and

ashes of pioneering, and the people too waste and ash, with the inner fire left out. There is still the pioneer tension as if something was still to be done, something conquered, something overcome, and there is no longer anything to conquer and no longer an enemy. I have walked around the streets of many small towns in Kansas. I have traveled over the country looking and looking. I lived my impressionable years in a Kansas corn village. In my youth as now I was looking for sustenance. I was looking for something to live on. I was trying to grow, to come alive.

In the mid-center of America a man can go blank for a long, long time. There is no community to give him life; so he can go lost as if he were in a jungle. No one will pay any attention. He can simply be as lost as if he had gone into the heart of an empty continent. A sensitive child can be lost too amidst all the emptiness and ghostliness.

I am filled with terror when I think of the emptiness and ghostliness of mid-America. The rigors of conquest have made us spiritually insulated against human values. No fund of instinct and experience has been accumulated, and each generation seems to be more impoverished than the last.

Look at the face of the Middle Westerner and you know he has been nourished in a poor soil without one day of good growing weather.

Yet there is the land abundant, in seasons. I have looked and looked at the land. The symbols of this country are winter, the departure of the year, the "death of all sweet things." It is the symbol of man's foreboding and his birth and his death. Life is not embodied. It is either just dying or being born. Who can tell? All our Americans have had this anxiety of life at the low ebb. I had it in my youth and still have it, a sickening anxiety like a disease, and all in that small town where I lived had it. It was limned on their faces like the ravages of some plague, some mysterious unmentioned disease of which we were all suffering. The sun leaving the earth and a terrible insecurity at the bottom of every man's soul, fears, dangers, hardships known and unknown as if one were never going to live to maturity, the days so tenuous in substance, a sheer fabric of horror and the town falling to pieces with its rotten wooden houses, and the gray shredded faces, and the place a horror, out of the world, doomed. I could not bear to get up in the morning after the winter solstice, as if some malignant power were in the air, the dim, dim faces, the blank interior of the continent, the winter madness coming on, the winter death, the sun leaving the great dark continent, the black, cold prairies, the shocks of corn desolate in the fields, the earth upturned in the cold sunlight, the smell of loam, the dark fields jagged and turned to the cold, the cattle wading through the black frozen mud and the wild embodied wind of the prairies like a presence among the fields.

The terrifying beauty too of the plains, the black stiff trees shadowless, the soft shadowless ice-world curving beneath the shadowless sky. Boys tracking down the valley, gophers hanging from their belts, gopher tails from their stocking caps. Men swathed in woolens watching the eastbound train. A hunter coming into the village, a rabbit hanging from his arm, the blood dropping from its eyes. The farm houses silent in the gullies, in the low curve of plain. The horses in the frozen corn. The smoke of the little brush trees in a mist of frost. The white earth sloping and still, the leaden sky, all things closed, no vista, no shaking out, no revelation. Where has life gone that there is no fire and no shadow?

I was born on these prairies while the land was lying low in this mid-winter solstice, lying low like this and dreaming. It curves now in low, long swells lying stark in the blue frost, so strong, so spare. Men come out of the wooden houses. I see their naked red arms, their hulking shoulders, their stubborn stocky heads. They run from the house to the barn, ducking their heads against the wind. These meaty men live in this delicate world, their bloody lives, and are looked upon by the rabbit, the prairie dog, and once the deer.

What does an American think about the land, what dreams come from the sight of it, what painful dreaming? Are they only money dreams, power dreams? Is that why the land lies desolate like a loved woman who has been forgotten? Has she been misused through dreams of power and conquest?

Anyhow the awful imprecations of the land lie heavily on the guilty white spirit. Remember the sadness and innate depression of Lincoln as symbolic. He was naturally a lover, but he never loved the land, though he walked miles over it, slept and lived on it, and buried the bodies of those he loved in it; and yet he was never struck with that poetry and passion that makes a man secure upon his land, there was always instead this convulsion of anxiety, this fear.

One night, in late fall, driving back from the country

our car stalled. The low dusk had come down over the prairies deepening and deepening around us like water and it was rather frightening too, because the distances became illusive and that strange emptiness and fear that no one admits were in the air. We were stalled in the road in front of the Simonsons' and, sensing our nearness, the Mrs. stood in the door and he came swinging his long frame through the dusk down the lane to us. Their house was a wooden one, shambling, behind a windbreak of trees, and the barns were better than the house and the stock better than the people.

"Hello," he called, and his voice sounded far away as if it echoed and was lost in the hollowness of the prairies.

"And John," his wife called, and we could not see her, "you'd better not go out without your coat." In that voice of the Yankee woman nagging her men.

Simonson came up to us and we saw his face and his tall Yankee body, the angular disjointed body Lincoln had.

"What's the matter? Stalled?" he said grinning, but he encompassed us with no warmth. He was simply curious and looked at us from a distance. I looked at his emaciated body with its hint of sickness like a stubborn, sturdy, thwarted tree, yet with a certain tenderness in it too. I remembered Lincoln's body, looking at Simonson; and again the old mystery presented itself in the underworld dusk of the phantom prairie world, the mystery of the slim tenuous Yankee body, hard and gawky like a boy's, never getting any man suavity in it, but hard and bitter and stubborn, always lanky and ill-nourished, surviving bitterly.

"Well," he said, suddenly gentle and impersonal, "that's too bad." And there was really a sad gentleness about him, so that I couldn't help liking him despite the acrid, bitter odor of the body, the slight warped sparseness of it that repelled, and yet the gawky tenderness. Lincoln too had this—the loose frame, the slight droop, the acrid, bitter power and tenuosity, the sense of hanging on in bad seasons, of despondency from lack of nourishment, that well-known Yankee form and the mystery of it, the strong, deep, lanky chest, so powerful but so withdrawn and gnarled, and the sudden tenacious sentimental sympathies, that would start wars for quixotic idealisms, provoke assassins' bullets and leave a wife embittered and maddened a little, left out always, never wholly warmed at that breast, the flesh never really warm and hanging from the tree of life, always a little acrid and ghostly, and the tenderness not enough to warm. And the anxiety always cooling the blood, making it spectral, the Yankee anxiety about something that leaves its mark on the face, on the skeleton, in the blood.

"Well," he said, scratching his ear and looking at us from his long, sorrowful face, "you better come in, hadn't you? You can come in if you want to . . ." The far, desolate slopes of the prairie were now invisible and the chill came down around us on the black land. Simonson began to talk to us as we walked over the black land and the horizon swung in its wide circle around us, and he went on talking in that sepulchral voice, as if he were the only man in the world, a far, lone man at an outpost, just waiting to move on, to move back, to move. There was his familiarity, his heartiness and the insensitive body, and his will set on not caring, not thinking, not attending to life at all but just to tramp blankly on from minute to minute in a vacuum.

We went toward the tumbling buildings so temporary and lost. There were no stars now the darkness had come, no North Star, no guide, and Simonson talking in a void, the last man on the frontier, a far, lone man at an outpost, waiting to move on, to move back, to move. . . .

We rarely went out of the town alone. In groups we sometimes went to some known place for picnics, usually where a stream made the prairies more gracious. But usually we went walking only a little way out of the town, as if we were besieged, surrounded by some mysterious forces. I remember feeling frightened at first stepping out of the close town onto the prairie, so wide with the wide sky opening away. . . . But I did not go out often alone.

There was an Irish family I knew who lived out a few miles from town. They were lazy and enjoyed themselves, and were considered somehow immoral by the townspeople. All the foreigners in the town were isolated by their gaiety, the festivals, easy love and birth. They were always attractive to me. The foreign girl prostitutes, the great Polish woman who kept a "house," where the college boys went and whose name we were forbidden to speak. I liked her body, so rich and loose, and her broad-hipped lazy walk. The acrid Yankee body is a hard thing to live with, always ungiven, held taut for some unknown fray with the devil or the world or the flesh. These illicit women, so menacing, were the only ones at that time who could wear bright colors.

This Irish family, Irish and goaty, came to town on Saturday, and I liked to ride out with them. They had large earthy, loose faces. We rode in a wagon through the hard, tight Kansas cold, the ruts frozen so hard our teeth rattled—no snow, just the frozen bald earth and the black scrub trees. The house was a little white house sitting on the top slope of the prairie. It was dirty and derelict. The inside would be cold and we would be cold, our hands and legs chapped and raw. Out of every window we could see the desolate cold prairie and the wind over it, the frozen stiff corn in the fields. At last there would be a fire in the stove, the lamps would be lighted. There was no evidence of any one living in the house, there were chairs, beds, adequate things, but it was like a camp, no idols, no tokens of intimate life. And then Mrs. Kelly would fry the thick fat pork and cook the potatoes in their jackets, and then we would eat in the lamplight, grinning at each other in that wild, wild way they had, and making jokes, prodding each other slyly and eating the rich pork and gravy, too rich and porky, no wine, no grace, just the greasy, porky meal with the raucous plain loping outside to the dismal horizon and this sly human grinning at each other, the sly grin of the Irish goaty faces, bewildered too but chewing a good cud of life somehow that they had brought with them over a black sea.

I am baffled to know the meaning of people in the Midwest towns. Lewis has not been right. He has portrayed their grimaces, a seeming reality, but still only their faces in a mirror. Anderson of course has apprehended them with love, but that too has left out a great deal.

I was hungering then, a-hunger and a-thirst. So were others. The whole communal organism suffered perhaps. One individual is only an articulated sensitive point for the great herd suffering. I went about the streets looking and looking, and what I saw seemed to be without pith or meaning, dark and spectral. And every one peering through the strange air of a new continent perhaps saw the same thing, the outward busy, strenuous life and the pithless core, the black abyss. . . . Perhaps it is inevitable that in a new country communication must be muffled and silent, that there is just a babbling on the surface, a genial, meaningless babbling, and that the real reciprocation must be in silence. Frontiersmen have put themselves aside.

So the only time the reality is revealed, the terrible surface torn aside, is after some violence. Violence somehow stirs up the deadly becalmed surface, breaks open the body. There was always excitement in cyclones—the darkness, the wind from another world, the delicious terror as if at last something would be expounded—even death, a real death, and then the great genii appearing on the becalmed horizon, approaching the marooned town, so that everything started to a kind of horrific reality, impressing its life through the ghostly maze, a hand lifted in terror, widened eyes, people running, screaming, embracing each other, waking from a dream, as if from a long, terrible journey, and the excitement afterward, the eye still widened, the hand uplifted, the heart accelerated, streets swarming, trees felled, houses upended, graves revealed, bones upturned, bones of Indians, the bones of French, Spanish, those who had been dead long in the land. The talk for days—"It took all the buttons off Sam Marvis' coat. Can you beat that? Yes, sir, he lay down in the field and the goldarned thing ripped the buttons off his coat. . . ." A visitation from a pagan world it was. But gradually the excitement would wear away, the strong cotton insulation of emotion would muffle it.

You look and look and you cannot see life anywhere apparent, only in bitterness, and spareness sold out for that neat, hygienic and sterile success that we all must have. There are whispers that so-and-so is doing this or that, but violence must erupt the awful lethargy, the fading away of the soul.

Once on Saturday when the town was crowded with farmers, and their wives were marketing in the thick black mud, a man shot a woman on Main Street. The woman was a young woman with gold hair, legendary as she lay dead, and she was standing looking into Stevens' Millinery Shop at a hat she probably coveted very much. And suddenly this man, her lover, jealous over a small thing, ran down the street brandishing a gun. Every one on the street stopped, a man fixing the bridle of his horse, a woman with an orange in her hand; and the distraught man stopped, took aim, and shot his sweetheart straight through the heart. She crumpled up, still looking at the hat, without a sound, and then while the man still stood with the bridle and the woman with the orange uplifted, he turned the gun upon himself and shot himself straight through the temple and fell in the street. For a moment no one moved. Every one stood as if bewitched. Something had happened. There it stood on Main Street, an ancient Thing. Then there was an eddying and rapid movement like dammed water let loose and the torrent broke in every breast–the townspeople broke in around the two and looked upon them in their own blood. The whole town was submerged by this torrent then. It broke in every breast and bound us all together. We turned like somnambulists looking at each other at last, not as ghosts distant and distraught, but now bound together alive, knowing ourselves alive.

There was something about it like a purging. A woman comes across the road to borrow some baking powder, and there is tenderness in her as she clicks her tongue, "The poor young things . . ." and something in the female blood wakens to think of love being like that.

And the men gather at the street corners and talk, and the close, dark knot of human form is woven close together–they no longer straggle, stand unwoven, apart, they stand close together, welded together in the lines of their bodies, their heads leaning close, for one of their kind has felt something and let it ripen and come to expression.

The town is woven in this lovely dream. The children, round-eyed, whisper together. The women gather. The men gather. Men and women draw closer to each other in the night. Love awakens in the town. Every one is drawn into the great warp of myth.

The whole village files into the church passing the two coffins where the two lovers lie together now. Something has been said now for the whole town. It's an expurgation, a catharsis. Women embrace each other and weep for their own sorrows. Men are hearty and gentle, meeting each other on the street, and for a moment looking through the mist, apprehending each other.

The day of the joint funeral is a holiday. The air is

rich with meaning, the streets look no longer harried and idiotic. They have meaning now, the black houses have meaning, the church, the steeple, the railroad station. These are now places where the human scene is enacted, where there might be great feelings, shedding of the blood even. The sun pours down and it is good to be a man and a woman. Something has happened. May it never be forgotten!

But it is forgotten. The lethargy looms again, everything closes up, the streets are as they were before, and men become again only traders, movers, buyers, sellers, farmers.

Another violence—the revival. The evangelist would be a strange man, often handsome. The young girls would stand in a bright group, twittering as he came into town, shying off yet eyeing him and he them. The boys would watch him going down Main Street. The matrons asked him to their tables. There were dreams of him in the night. Even my grandmother got excited. The opening night of the revival there was always something special on our table, the dinner was a little better, there was the hint of rite and symbol.

I never saw her so excited as upon these nights of revival, so happy, so contented. She was like an actress on her opening night. She put on her best dress. She was affectionate even, and my grandmother never kissed us. She was embarrassed by any excess of feeling and had a way of turning down her lips bitterly. She had that acrid, bitter thing too about her body, a kind of sourness as if she had abandoned it. It was like an abandoned thing, perhaps it had not been occupied. The Puritans used the body like the land as a commodity, and the land and the body resent it. She never took a bath except under her shift. Hearing her move about her room alone I always wondered what she was doing, so bodyless, with that acrid odor as if she had buried her body, murdered and buried it, and it gave off this secret odor revealing the place where it lay.

Yet she was faithful in her duties, dogged in her service to those she loved, but it seemed to be a sacrifice without joy, a love without passion, and her children, like the children of every one, seemed to have been born without contact.

Pleasure of any kind was wicked, and she never lay down in the daytime even when she was dreadfully tired. It would have been a kind of licentiousness to her to have done so.

The coldness in her and severity gave her that sense of always spying on others, and she did have that passionate curiosity that comes in people marooned in any way from life by spiritual or physical illness. But religion was her theater, her dance, her wine, her song. Every night sitting bolt upright in her strong stiff body she sang these haunting hymns, picking them out in dull chords on the untuned piano. It was a long time before I knew that they were her love songs, the only ones she and others had. With a brilliant husband and four children, still she was mysteriously marooned, unliving and ghostlike without abundance or contact, without bloom in her body, without essential growth or maturity.

The evening would come down soft and sweet, and we would set out for the revival, my grandmother very stiff and self-conscious in her best silk, walking ahead, her black Bible in her gloved hands, and smiling that little smirk at her neighbors as if she knew something about them. Other people would be going sedately toward the little steepled church, and the young girls, arm in arm, and the boys together standing outside the church door, the boys standing brazenly watching the girls go in. Then they would come in a gang and sit in the balcony, looking down at the girls who would be in an agony of self-consciousness.

We would all greet each other, each thinking that the other had every cause to repent, but still more cordial than at ice-cream socials. Then every one in his best clothes in the packed brilliant church, the stir of starched clothes, the smell of violet water, and the bright faces of the choir so rosy, looking for the preacher. At last he would come out, melancholy and conscious, and sit down not knowing what to do with his hands, an unknown man to them all, a stranger from another part come into the town to stir them; and they were ready to be stirred, their close ungiven bodies ready to be mysteriously stirred by this stranger.

When I joined the church there was a red-headed Irishman who was the evangelist, a man of monstrous amorous vitality which he threw into his sermons, a great, wild vitality wonderful to behold and a silver Irish tongue too, so that he broke all the bitterness asunder, the silvery words breaking over the landlocked, corroded people. He was a fine actor, and had a fine roll to his words and a great sonorous natural cadence that added richness to our terse Yankee speech for many days after.

Then the hymns, and still the congregation, awkward, unwelded, and the wild-bucking youth in the balcony giving a feeling of something a little dangerous.

Then he rose and put back his thick hair, just a little longer than the men in the town wore theirs, and he let his great words have their way, flow over the hungry people, and they were unafraid because they were packed so closely, because it was impersonal and the great words fell like fruit upon famine–*This is my body ... I have died to save you ... Come unto me all ye who are heavy laden and I will give you rest*–and women who had never given one whit of love to their husbands or children let tears of love spring to their eyes and wept quite unashamed, and the young girls were hushed and the giant men sat dumb, shamefaced, and the boys with their mouth frozen in a guffaw. The close-weeping pack again welded, brought together, moving close in lovely formation.

"Let us sing the hymn of invitation. Come to your Savior now. Acknowledge him, my sisters, my brothers." Oh, the weeping now! "Come to Jesus who died for love of you."

"Oh, comfort me with apples, stay me with flagons." The breaking open at last. The choir singing, O sweetly, wondrously: "Jesus, lover of my soul, let me to thy bosom fly...." And these people without another love song, untinged by humor. The weeping women going to the altar and the men being pushed and herded and some weeping.

Afterward, leaving the bright turmoil of the church, outside the boys lined up waiting to take the girls home and the night sweeter than a nut, at last with the stars now with meaning, the town now close and beloved, broken open with love, and all the rich juices flowing out as from some ripe sweet fruit. And the girls in ecstasy and love. And all filled with awe for those who had confessed, and the newly saved silent and tearful, and every one tender with them. And the closed houses breaking open, cracking open like nuts, and the lovely faces looking out, and Jesus with his lovely face too, and the obscure, the terrible ecstasy over the town.

But the revival ends too and the stranger leaves the town. The sinners forget they have been saved. The great mid-continent vacuum swallows everything again. Everything is quiet until the corn-husking, and that means work and competition.

Oh, Kansas, I know all your little trees. I have watched them thaw and bud and the pools of winter frozen over, the silos and the corn-blue sky, the wagon-tracked road with the prints of hoofs, going where? And the little creeks gullying with delicate grasses and animals, the prairie dog, the rabbit, and your country with its sense of ruin and desolation like a strong raped virgin. And the mind scurrying like a rabbit trying to get into your meaning, making things up about you, trying to get you alive with significance and myth.

I have seen the spring like an idiotic lost peasant come over your prairies scattering those incredibly tiny flowers, and the frozen earth thaw to black mud, and a mist of greening come on the thickets, and the birds coming from the South, black in the sky, and farmers coming to the village through the black mud.

I have seen your beauty and your terror and your evil.

I have come from you mysteriously wounded. I have waked from my adolescence to find a wound inflicted on the deep heart. And have seen it in others too, in disabled men and sour women made ugly by ambition, mortified in the flesh and wounded in love.

Not going to Paris or Morocco or Venice, instead staying with you, trying to be in love with you, bent upon understanding you, bringing you to life. For your life is my life and your death is mine also.

No Wine in His Cart

For Doris

Stella jiggled the phone, the connections in these rural telephones were always difficult. Why, why weren't they in town when something important was happening? And no papers until tomorrow morning. Such a hot day too ... "Hello ... Hello ... I want to get Minneapolis ... Yes, yes, yes, the stock exchange. What is the matter– Arnold Gregory–the stock exchange."

Stella looked at Henrietta, the housekeeper, who stood in the door. The two women looked at each other while Stella listened at the phone. Henrietta seemed to be listening too. "I was wondering how the strike is going," Henrietta said. The two women looked at each other. "That's what I am trying to do, get my husband," Stella said. Henrietta looked at her. She thinks I don't know anything about strikes, Stella thought, my father was in many strikes. Both women looked out the window down the hill to the lake. It was such a hot day, the hills stood in the heavy tawny sunlight. The corn was ripening in the garden, the long silky leaves shining quite still like green swords in the sun. Stella watched the tiny fishermen on the lake and listened to the small sounds in the black space of the phone. From where she was sitting at the phone she could look straight from their glassed room down both sides of the hill; on one side sat the fishermen, on the other side beyond the tennis court she could see the Sicilian wine cart Arnold's father had brought back from Italy. All morning she had looked, from time to time, at the fishermen sitting quite still on the glassy lake and not once had they pulled up a fish. They looked burned to a char with their black poles out over the shimmering water. She watched, but they never once pulled in a fish. Weren't there any fish in his lake? it wasn't possible. "Henrietta, I wonder if there are any fish in the lake?" she said, holding down the receiver. "I'll have to call again, why is there no answer?" The silence was thick with heat. It seemed as if something were about to spring out of it right behind your shoulders, as if someone were spying in the still heat.

"I hope they catch something," Henrietta said. Stella looked at the fishermen. "I know that they are pretty hard up, they're probably fishing for their supper."

Stella's heart gave a start. For some reason it had not occurred to her that they were not playing a game, fishing for sport. "Hello, hello," she said, "yes, yes, yes, that's my connection. Hello, hello!" she strained every nerve to hear, the voice came muffled, from far, far away. "Arnold, Arnold," she cried, "hello, yes, this is Stella. Listen, I want to know something. I want to find out about the strike—yes, the strike." He mumbled something she couldn't hear, then repeated it. "Yes, yes, this evening. I know but I want to know now. What, what?" She shook the phone in exasperation. "I can't hear a word," she shouted. "What? I know I'm shouting but I want to hear. What? Yes. Hello. Hello. He's gone!" A terrific rage swept through her, why had he hung up like that? Why had he mumbled? She felt like screaming, like tearing the handsome room apart. "Get whatever you want for supper, Henrietta, I don't care what it is, and I don't want to take the baby out this afternoon, I don't want to see anybody. If anybody calls I'm not here. I'm not here at all."

When Henrietta left she stood in the room like an imbecile and stared at the bowl of Chinese waterlilies. She looked out the windows down the handsome lawn, the lake, the tennis court, everything, all made by Arnold. Oh, Stella has made a good marriage, an excellent marriage, what a break for a girl like that, a Yale man, plenty of money. It was a break to marry money. Still those fishermen did not catch a thing. Arnold had made the lake and had put fish in it but perhaps they were all gone, yes, they must be, she had not seen them draw in a single fish.

Yes, she had everything she wanted, the heir to the Gregory millions lay upstairs, about to have his dinner, but she didn't want to see him today. You went along for days, did things, had fun, then suddenly you collapsed. You could not move an eyelash; everything was meaningless and you thought way back six months before and you wondered what you had been doing all that time and you could think of a dress you had gotten, something good to eat, some conversations like a dream and for the rest, gone, gone without a trace.

She had to get out of the house, so she went down towards the old wine cart which she loved. Every little man so gaily painted on it reminded her of her own father. The great colored wheels were bright in the sun. She climbed up and looked at the signs of the Zodiac painted in the center, and everywhere were the faces of men like her father's—ancient, long, forgotten workmen picking grapes, carving, hammering, carrying fagots, and women nursing babies, cooking, bending, lifting. A gaiety seemed all around the cart, you could feel the surge and push of many men and an active abundant life of bustle still around the cart. Why had Arnold's father brought it back from Sicily, had it meant something to him? Or was it only a curious possession? When she was lonely for the raucous, hand to mouth, terrible and yet abundant life of her parents she went down to the wine cart to look at all the curious little painted men, the wide mouths, the workman's body like her father's. The body of a workman was the same everywhere. The cart was covered with the tiny bright figures in every posture and attitude, striking an anvil to shoe a horse, gathering, treading the grapes–the same sensitive body moulded close to its labor, a worn tool.

She sat up bolt in the bright sun. Why had Arnold's body been distasteful to her, his white hands, his white narrow chest, self-conscious, without use. Making money never made use of a man's body, the smell of it got on him. Perhaps a woman never really could love the body of a money-making man. Could it be true? She put her hand down on the burning wood of the wine cart and cried. The sun lay warm on her hair, shoulders, in the pit of her back. She did not know when she stopped crying but she lay still in the bottom of the wine cart and the warm sun seemed to drown her. There was not a sound, everything stood quite still. In the spring when they had come out from the city there had been larks everywhere making the air seem like water for carrying the sound that came up out of the misty spring like bubbles breaking over them but since the heat and no rain, there hadn't been a bird sound. There was not a bird now. It was still as a mouse.

There seemed to be a presence creeping on the lawn. She thought if she sat up and looked she would see some colossal force without face slowly rise up the lawn, pluck the house like a vile weed and crush it and leave the bald pate of the hill with the trees silently growing. She could bear it no longer and sat up, her head seemed thrust up into a golden syrup dark in the heat and she could see every leaf on the tree distinctly. She had the impression of spying on something, playing a game.

It seemed to her, in half drowse, that the fishermen far down below must be pulling in fish when she wasn't looking. Arnold had everything, he certainly would have fish in his lake. An awful grin seemed to split her face. She thought if she would look away and then back quickly she would see them pulling in a fish but there they sat as if carved out of burnt wood, smoking a little in the heat.

Stealthily she looked down the lawn. Arnold's young shrubs and trees seemed to be wilting. The house had been a wedding present so the ancient trees stood outside the sharp cut trimness of the paths and hills, and beyond the brush and the strong upmounding hills, with their soft fur like on animals. She felt as if spying on them. She always felt that Arnold's shrubs and things belonged to the social world and not to the natural one anyway. She tried to see into the trees to see if she might spy a bird waiting for rain but she could only see the heat far inwards permeating the tree so it seemed to swim in the dancing air.

She felt curiously as if she were spying, as if some

little peekhole opened up and she would see into something, like once she had sat on the back stairs looking through the butler's door at a tea, now she lay down again and let herself spy on Arnold, and she saw his fine surface but what was in him? She had a great excitement as if about to draw something out. You could go on living with Arnold for a thousand years, pleasantly, even gaily and you would never know anything about him, you would never have a quarrel, you would never grow into something different, even into a beast. It was as if he were manufactured like his silly little estate. She felt excited as if she had discovered something. The perfect husband, she thought, he is the perfect husband and no husband at all. In the heavy summer stillness it was as if her mind had shouted this and she waited to be shot for treason but the world did not shift nor move, the furry hills, tawny, curved, ached towards the sun.

She stood up as if drunk, in the wine cart, and recalling some gaminry of her childhood, she spat at the house.

Arnold came home at six. He didn't look as if the heat had touched him. She seemed to see him too clearly, as if she had never seen him before. He kissed her and she drew back but he didn't notice. He smiled at her. He carried himself very tall as if he was always being what he thought a man ought to be, a Yale type perhaps. "Listen, Arnold for heaven's sake not so close, it's so hot and I'm all in, there hasn't been a breath of air."

"Look at those fishermen fishing down there," he said.

"Haven't I been looking at them all afternoon?" He moved away and looked annoyed at her.

"This heat is unheard of," he said, "such a prolonged spell."

She felt she still had one eye closed as if cunningly spying on him. Yes, she thought, I've married above me. Those fishermen can't be really fishing, it's all part of the game. "Won't they catch anything?" she said.

"What is it, dear?"

"Those fishermen . . ."

"Next year I'll have to bring in some more fish."

"You mean put fish in the lake?"

"Yes," he flicked over the evening paper in his long white hands.

Stella suddenly wanted to strike him. She walked over and looked out the window, a purple haze was rising from the sun-drunk earth. Arnold made an exclamation, she turned surprised and caught a close, cruel expression on his small face. She cried out without thinking, "Arnold, what is it? What is the matter?"

"A great deal is the matter," he said in a terrible precise way. "We are going to fix them."

"The strikers," she cried. The great change in her own feeling had made her forget them.

"Yes," he said, "I was at a meeting this very afternoon. The citizens are going to organize and break the picket line. They should deputize every citizen of the town and go down there."

"The citizens . . ." she repeated, her blood going cold in her. She had never seen the man sitting across from her, never known him.

"But, Arnold, who are the citizens?"

"Every respectable citizen," he repeated, his face lean and mean. "All of them."

"Why, Arnold, I never saw you like this, haven't they a right to organize?"

"They're not running our business. We'll show them who is the head of this country."

She thought of all his humanitarian ideas, the right of assemblage, Jeffersonian democracy about which he was fond of talking, but she said nothing. Something seemed to stand visible in the room between them at last, to emerge out of the heat. The fishermen were still sitting in the dusk fishing for their supper. The emergence was so clear that she thought she would scream.

Henrietta stood in the doorway announcing supper. Arnold got up, she walked in front of him but their life was over, the doorway was unreal, and the mahogany table with its summer cloth. She sat down like a ghost and he sat opposite, his face flushed, his eye narrowed coldly. He went on to tell her about the meeting, about the battle of Bull Run there had been that afternoon between the police and the strikers. He told about a street full of men standing side by side like a tide and cracking the bulls over the head, driving them back, stopping trucking completely and the women stood side by side with them . . .

"The women?" she cried, "were there women there?" Her poor mother had wanted her to marry above her.

"Many women," he said, "even young girls. It was disgusting. They probably brought in a lot of thugs from Chicago, beat up the policemen in the performance of their duty, to protect life and property."

"The women were there," she said, then they weren't marrying above them anymore.

Henrietta brought the salad. She was listening to

everything. Stella could tell by her dilated eyes. She must try and keep her temper. The green fluffy leaves sat on the salad plates from Carcassonne. Why, half the things they had were peasant things, everyone brought them back from Europe. There on the dishes from Carcassonne was the same tiny figure, the little workman's figure, dogged, real, bending now under a load of fagots. On every plate he stood bending a little with the fagots on his back, his black hat pulled down over his face. She saw thousands of him—multiplied.

"We're going in there tomorrow," he was saying.

She wanted to penetrate, to destroy him. "That's hideous," she cried. "That's dastardly, where's all your fine words, the right of free speech and assemblage, the right to unionize, what's come of it all? You know they don't get much. I know how much they get. I've known it all my life. . . ."

He looked at her coldly. "You'd better go to your room," he said.

"I won't," she cried.

Then he said in a low cutting voice, "You'd be in that mess yourself if I hadn't married you."

"Yes," she said coldly. The room seemed to dissolve in worm-eaten wood. The three fishermen still sat in the dusk, waiting. They might get up in anger and come towards the house. All the figures from the wine cart might spring out and come stealthily up the hill and surround the house.

She said to him, jeering, "Are you really going down there tomorrow, all you businessmen to fight the strikers?"

"Yes," he said, "we are."

"Then you'll get hurt," she said with satisfaction.

"Why do you think so?"

"I know so," she said, "you can't beat them."

"We'll beat them all right," he said. "We've got equipment. We're going to buy arms and tear gas." It angered her bitterly that he should be excited about this destruction as he had never been about anything before.

"You'll get hurt," she said bitterly, "you better mind. You'll get hurt."

"We'll show them," he said.

"Yes, you'll show them," she said and an awful laughter tore through her, for she knew the curious deep life in those many men, how all the many hungers could rise up. Why had she given up her many hungers for this? "You ..." she cried in contempt knowing his pale body as if it had been dead under water and she shook with humiliation and grief to know how she had been with him, borne him a child. "You're through," she cried, "you're through, there's no wine in your cart!" The fishermen started to row towards shore.

"Stella," he said, shaking her.

"That's all right," she said. "I know now. And you're lost, you're lost already. You better not go down there tomorrow, if you care for your poor hide."

"I'll go," he said with his little courage.

"You'll get hurt," she said and she thought, I hope he is killed. I hope he can die!

Fable of a Man and Pigeons

There was once a man who felt better in Chicago after having fed pigeons. If you happened to be there by the fountain when he came with corn in his pockets for them, you saw a workman walk towards you with a very delicate happy swing to his body and a look of extraordinary pleasure on his face. Outside of this he looked like workmen look all over the world, a certain submission in them that is at once terrible and beautiful but beside this, there was on this man's face a look of pain and delicacy and at the same time pleasure as he stood with his hands out, the pigeons flying in excitement around him.

There was the earth somewhere underneath Chicago but the heavy labyrinth and steel darkness weighed on men, then this man would walk a great way out of the city coming alone, confused by the closeness and blindness of steel things and mineral noises and suddenly like coming out of a cave straight upon water he would emerge on the lake front, and the pigeons in a sweet confusion of flight were upon him, hurling their bodies through the glistening sun, whirling skyward in close formation, settling again around him, strutting after him or uneasy on his shoulders.

A very unusual thing had happened to Yasha Raskob, that is, in itself it was nothing but it turned out that such a small happening changed his whole life. Years later when he looked down at his hand where the wound had healed he was reminded of something. It became vague later but the scar never went away and it always reminded him of something...

He lived in a wooden house on State Street, up three flights of stairs. He had a wife with a shrill voice who thought he ought to be doing better. No matter what success he might have achieved she would never have been satisfied. She was dissatisfied about something very deeply, but it was really something more than simply how much money they had, but neither of them ever knew what it was exactly.

For twenty years he had worked in a button factory so his fingers were rough on the edges and he began to feel that everything he touched was hard and blunt. Beside his wife he knew no one. In a modern factory you might work your whole life and really not know a soul. Meeting in the lavatory – "How are you Raskob ... how are you?" Where can that get with a man? So gradually he felt as if he were being cemented in a space that just held him so he had to shout to make his own wife hear him.

It was true that they rarely spoke to each other normally. They spoke not at all or they shouted as if they were on separate islands and could never at best hear what the other was saying. When he came home, up the three flights of stairs, passing the many odors of cooking, there she would be looking out at him going over old letters, photographs from her life on an Iowa farm. How she had married Raskob neither of them knew. She had thought he had money, he had thought her beautiful, been swept off his feet, and after that rocket had burst it had all gone out and she had been a stranger to him crouching in the many dark rooms they rented, looking at him with hatred, or shrilling like a parrot when he drank their money.

He looked at her sometimes wondering where the girl was buried in her. But it was like a death and at last he thought that the girl was completely decomposed and gone in the wind. He thought of her as the old woman but he did not think of himself as old. He suffered too, from the death of their love, having her in the room like an old bird with her beak in his vitals. So at night he got into the habit of walking around the city alone, leaving her to wait his return, for she had no other life than her anger towards him. Walking by himself he had strange fancies...

Then one day something happened that changed his whole life. The machine at which he had sat for so long, like a patient animal who suddenly goes mad, bit his hand, tore it apart right out of the casing of flesh and he was laid off with pay and hospital expenses and for the first time since he was a boy he had leisure in the daytime.

No one can understand what this means who has not sat for that many years in a button factory all the time the sun is shining. Now he had no master, he could sleep until nine, then he could get up, wash and dress in his Sunday clothes and go out like a man of leisure, going about the city looking and listening. A strange thing happened, what he heard and what he saw took on a different color. It was as if for the moment he walked outside of life and could really see it like a bubble hanging in the midst of creation and disaster. It was at that time that he began going to the park to feed the pigeons every day. At first he took only stale bread, then he bought something better, a pocketful of corn.

It was then too he got that look of pleasure on his face and of pain too. His face was like a mask that has been set for years and then begins suddenly to change. His "old woman" saw it and she was maddened thinking that he was escaping her. He sat at his meals with that frightening delicate look that shut him away from her. She began to scream at him, "Look what has happened to us. Look at me. What has happened? See what you have done to me." One night the neighbors all came running, doors opened and slammed, there were knocks on their door, because she was screaming at him, "You have murdered me. You have murdered me . . ." And he could not believe that he had murdered her. "No," he said coldly his face becoming stern. "You have murdered me . . ." The people went back to their beds when they could see no murder at all.

He got up and went down State Street past a flower shop where he had seen a black car stop and fill a man with lead who stood there. He thought he would have to get among men, he would have to speak to someone. So he went into the Baptist mission and sat down amongst men who sat like vultures looking as if they lived off death, as if it hung in shreds from their mouths where they had eaten. They reminded him of his wife. He kept looking, wondering, wondering what men could say together so there would be more than just meetings . . . How are you? How are you? What if at such a question a man should say, I am dying, that's how I am . . . But no man would say that. A bum asked him for a light and he struck a match and stood dead before the other man and they didn't speak to each other at all.

He left and went down the canal through the sleeping markets with the smell of rotting vegetables. He felt a rebuff in every stone, something tearing men apart, some corrosion and wolfishness. Someone was running past the elevators, he heard the soft padded steps and he hid in the black shadow of a pillar. A man ran by close to him. Two other men came after. He could have touched them with his hand which he held close to his side. The sound of their steps passed him like a thunder; three men had run past him. He stood tense in the shadow isolated, alone, speechless.

He started back to his wife because she was the only one he knew and hate was better than nothing. The chill had got into his bones, and he darted like a fugitive from shadow to shadow or pulling in his shoulders close to his ribs he went, a dark figure through the moonlight that turned into stone as it struck steel. His cap made a shadow for a face lean and sad as if he brooded inwardly on a death that touched all men.

But when he got home he would not lie on the bed beside her, he lay down on the floor instead in a narrow space as if on a slab, with his arms pressed close to his side. The only life was the steady throbbing in his wounded hand.

The next morning to get away from her nagging— "A nice thing to go off and leave me . . . a nice thing," and then she cried as if the girl were crying out of those mad eyes—he went through the town and out to the lake front where he took bread from his pockets for the pigeons who flew about him lighting on his hands, on the white bandage, pecking from his palm with incisive beaks. He became wholly absorbed in looking at them, the close plumb eyes, the warm full bodies. He thought, how warm a bird is, putting his hand on the crouching feathered body.

Many people sat on the benches looking at him as he stood in the sun amidst the pigeons with that delicate smile on his lips. Suddenly for no reason in a suffocating confusion they would all rise with a noise of feathered flesh and circle about him so he felt about to swoon: then they flew back around him looking for a place to light, coming against him with their feathered wings. The terror of birds in their flight gave him a delicate passion and pleasure, something he had not felt since he was a young man. He felt as if he had not felt any heat of man or woman like the heat of the birds' bodies on his hands.

Fatigued from the pleasure he sat down on the bench and they walked about his feet, the females so down-drooping and modest, the fat males gorgeous, preening themselves, walking after.

Every day he could not wait to have his hand dressed and get back to the park and sit and watch them. As they mated he felt he should put his hand over them. Something unbearable came back into him. He stood up in the confusion of light and wind and the pigeons beat about him, trembling in balance like bodied light, then they all rose together whirring off and settling back again, pairing off. He looked at them through the white falling summer light smiling with pleasure. The old men on the benches ducked and the women put papers over their hats as they whirred over afraid of the narrow plumb eyes, the sharp beaks and the cruel rose feet and their swift cruel flight. Sometimes the wind blew whipping the spray from the fountain, putting everything in a wonderful confusion of birds and light and blowing water.

It seemed impossible a man could have so much flight and pleasure feeding pigeons in Chicago.

As he watched something rose in him pushing against his throat, some unbearable buried thing, as if a bird was inside him beating against his ribs, and was flying forever between the vaults of his body, beating its wings, unable to be set free.

He thought he would never go back to the mechanical world again, never go back to his machine, to his old life, to his wife bullying, driving, scolding.

He saw the wonderful splendor of the mating pigeons, their delicate approach, the thunder in their arched throats, the excitement in their bodies which for some reason made him think of the excitement of an orchard in blossom that he remembered from his youth in Russia.

One morning unable to bear it he actually ran through the streets up State Street. He had some vague idea of finding the girl he had married, the girl from Iowa, prairie dreaming, to touch her, waken her. Perhaps she too thought of herself as young. Perhaps there in that wrinkled flesh lived the young girl who remembered orchards blooming.

He ran and ran and everyone looked at him, some smiling. He didn't look like a man running from a murder. For a moment perhaps they all saw the boy running as he had run once naked by the river Bug to catch up with the sun. It might be possible that men coming out of the Wrigley building to have lunch and turning to watch him running may have seen something quite clearly for a moment.

Two steps at a time he took to their room and flung open the door and for a moment coming out of the flashing noon light he could see nothing. He smelled the close odor in the dank room. Then he saw there was no one there. Panting he sank into a chair and sat hearing his heart gradually slow, his breath dim, the color go out of his flesh. His wounded hand began to throb like a bell ringing and he sat holding it in his well one.

In an hour the door opened and there stood the old woman. He leaped up. He had been feeling quite calm but at the sight of her leaped up and grabbed her spilling the packages she carried. A look of greed came on her. She lived on their passions of hate like food. "Where have you been, you old hag," he cursed, and slowly with pleasure he began to beat her and every time he struck her a knife seemed to go through his hurt hand and once she took hold of the raw flesh slowly squeezing it.

Afterwards they clung together. They were like two people in mid-ocean on a raft seeing who would kill the other first and each knew the ghastly purpose.

Before dawn he got up, washed himself, and went out. He thought he would never come back. The sun came up through the midst of the avenue, over the steel cliffs. He thought he would walk out of town, out into the country, and that night he would sleep in the hay. Hay . . . he did not even know the word for it in English. But he could smell it. It had been spread on the floor for beds when they were children. Where were his father, mother, brothers, sisters . . . Lost . . . gone . . .

Was there no flight for men? for women?

He did not know how to get out of town. He thought he was caught in some cave. He knew the country, the fields of wheat, rye, barley, mustard must lie all around them but how to get to them, which way to start was beyond him. He sat down by the fountain; the sun came up. He did not care what happened.

The pigeons began to fly down for their breakfast. His pockets were empty and he did not want to see their delicate matings. He felt embarrassed because he had nothing. He got up and the pigeons all followed like royal beings of some kind and he felt shy. They came cooing, strutting at his heels. He felt as if he disappointed them some way and it made him shy. He tried to shoo them back but they followed and he had a terror that they might walk right after him haunting him forever. He waved his hands and they rose and settled back again, one on his shoulder. He could see the bright single eye cocked at him. He felt bereft, hurt. One of them flew on his hand and suddenly he began striking out at them like a madman waving his arms. He felt the impact with a body and a pigeon half fell volplaning down and crouching there a moment. They rose and whirled off into the sky. He walked rapidly feeling he had struck them too.

He started to walk through the city, thinking that if he cut back through he would be more likely to come out the other side but he walked and walked for hours. When he got tired he saw himself going back to his wife, back to the factory, seeing all that forever and he could not do it. He kept walking and came to a park by afternoon where he lay down and slept. He thought he was sleeping beneath the shadow of flying night birds, out of the world. There was a bright confusion of wings, and unhuman eyes never closing and millions of flight feet. He forgot the machine. A wind blew in that world silently, a faint wind.

He woke feeling a wind going over him, and saw it go down between the trees lifting a piece of old paper, then up through the lifting foliage as if something had passed. He felt something had happened as if he had been removed a distance from the world that would never be traversed back again.

He got up and walked around the park, then he knew what he would do. He started back towards the city, found himself at the bottom of the stairs again, climbed up, opened the door into the stale room, felt his wife malignant, sleeping like some serpent in the darkness.

The next morning the doctor said his hand was cured, took off the bandage exposing the white flesh and he saw where it had mended. He would always have a scar where the flesh had been sewed together over the blood and bone. His hand was white as if it had been in some other world.

He looked at it turning it over and over. The next week he had to go back to the factory and there was his machine waiting for him.

His hand got the same as the other, that is, lost its unnatural whiteness, but the scar was always there and sometimes he looked at it and tried to remember something.

He never went again to feed the pigeons. As before it was sundown now when he got home and besides he had no stomach for it.

Sometimes on Sunday he walked down to the lake with his old woman and the pigeons flew towards them and she put a newspaper over her hat, then for some reason they would always quarrel.

"They won't hurt you . . ."

"You shut up . . . My only hat . . . God knows, I don't have many hats . . . Some women . . ."

A pang of sickness would come into his body seeing the pigeons flying, lifting, mating, in that delicate thunder of blooming. His hand would pain as if it opened again in the old wound and they would quarrel the whole afternoon.

A Hungry Intellectual

Andrew Hobbs was an intellectual. He continually said he was an intellectual, an idealist. Before the depression he had had a job as an advertising writer, and had a stenographer of his own, that's what he said. He was always telling us what a good position he had had and how he was getting on in the world. Of course he was just going into advertising until he got started with his writing, he said, but he seemed to get farther and farther into debt, so he never could stop his job. That was before the depression scooped him out, with not so much as a by-your-leave, and left him without any of the gadgets he had bought, and dumped him on the streets.

The first time I saw him he was talking against God down at Gateway Park, standing very tall, his narrow head showing above the crowd of workmen. The old gospel-monger was holding forth across the street, and Hobbs was talking Ingersoll atheism on the opposite corner, and he would take up a collection afterwards which would sometimes amount to even fifty cents. Anyhow he could eat off it. But he said he didn't really care for the collection, it was just the principle of the thing, if a person didn't pay for a thing they didn't appreciate it, even a few dimes like that.

I always had an awful time keeping the children quiet, waiting for the speaking to be over and the boys to come home to dinner. Karen was only two and Sybil just nine months. There was fifteen months between them. Somebody brought him over and introduced him and he stood back very modestly and tried to keep his shoes in the dark. He looked like he was trying to step back through a door that wasn't there. He seemed to be stepping back away from something, away from any one touching him so that his face and even his body seemed to have a receding look about them as if he would presently disappear into something behind him. For all that, he was well-meaning, anyone could see that. And he had his own pride.

When Karl introduced him, he took off his hat and bowed a little, like a Southern gentleman, and sure enough I found out he had been raised in Georgia, the lower middle class, always trying to get up further, always thinking themselves ascending a little on the social ladder and really descending frightfully from generation to generation. This continual lowering and defeat gave him a sad gentility. He took off his hat and bowed a little and seemed to recede.

Karl went back to the corner with the boys to distribute some leaflets about the mass meeting the next night, and Hobbs sat down in the car with me and politely asked about the children, but he was ignoring them. The pigeons walked around the feet of the unemployed men sitting in the park, getting the last breath of summer air before going to their flops. "You know," Hobbs said, "I don't have to do this."

"Listen!" I shouted at Karen, "sit still just a minute and I'll get you a cone. What?" I said.

"I graduated from the University of Georgia," he said delicately.

"Yeah? Listen!" I shouted between my teeth. "I'll get you a tooth brush with Mickey Mouse on it." I couldn't keep them quiet. Hobbs looked offended as if he had smelled something bad. He jerked up his pants over his knee and I could see his awfully white shanks and he had no socks on. He jerked down his pants again and I felt sorry because I could see his poor feet, in somebody else's shoes and one shoe had a big place like a carbuncle where the guy who had had them before kept his bunion.

"I don't know what I am going to do," I said. "I can't wait around at these meetings all the time because the milk gets sour."

He smiled abstractedly, and looked out past the tattered top of the Ford at the sky. He had a thin face. He looked hungry. I remember the way I had seen his pants bag down over his rumps as if he had filled them more at some time.

"Why don't you come along and have supper with us?" I said. "We're going to have a swell stew."

"Well," he said, vaguely, so very delicate and evasive, "I don't know, I was supposed to meet a fellow over here." He waved his long white hand. "I don't know I might ... Wait a minute ... I'll see if I can find him."

He swung his long thin shanks out the door. "O.K.," I said, swatting Sybil's hands so they wouldn't catch in the door. I watched him take a walk behind the statue of the unknown soldier, duck a few seconds on the other side and come back. He didn't have to meet anybody. He didn't have anybody to meet.

He came to our house often just about supper time. He

never came right in and had something to eat like others. He always stood vaguely in the door, and bowing a little, and my lord he got thinner and thinner until he seemed like a wraith and his pants hung on his poor shanks like an old sack. "Well, well," he would say, politely, "you're just having supper. No . . . no, I don't want to spoil your evening meal."

"We're just having supper," I would say. "Come on in and have supper."

"No. No," he would say, flapping his white hands. "I just ate." And he would brush his face off with his hands as if he had walked through cobwebs. He would sit on the step and we would whisper inside about it.

"I know he hasn't had any supper."

"The poor guy," Karl would say.

"Why doesn't he say . . . just say he's hungry and come in and eat."

"It's pride."

"My God, everyone is hungry."

"I know, but he's an intellectual."

"Ohhhhh!"

Then all who were eating would fall against each other sniggering.

"Shut up," I'd say. "He'll hear."

Afterwards, when the boys went out to the meeting, he'd come in sometimes and help me with the children. If I went out of the room for something, I could see that he took things off the table, and when I would come back, he wouldn't chew a bit but sit there smiling vaguely, with his mouth full of food, so I would have to go out again so he could chew it up.

He never once said he was hungry. He always had

mysterious places where he said he slept and ate. Yet we all knew that he slept at the mission and ate that slop. Lots of the boys saw him there, but he never said a word about it, never said that he did, as if not saying so made it not so.

He seemed to like better to be with me than with the boys. He was raised by women I guess and felt easier with them, and the boys made fun of his high-falutin' ideas. He would say all sorts of great high-sounding phrases he must have remembered from school. "We must all struggle," he would say, "life is progress." And yet he seemed neither to struggle nor to make any progress. You could see he felt fine when he was talking. I would feed the babies or change them for the night, and you could see in a few minutes he made the world a place it was easy for him to be in. He kept saying that change must come without violence, that it must be intellectual.

I said, "When you have a baby, birth is violent."

"No. No," he said. "Change must come from the intellect with understanding and non-violence, non-resistance."

"I don't think it's that way," I said. "From having a baby I think it's different. It comes out violently."

I could see him eyeing the last chop left on the plate. "Why don't you eat that chop?" I said. I wanted to give the bone to the baby to chew anyway; besides, one chop is nothing to fix another meal with.

He said, "Oh, I had plenty, plenty," and he went on talking, telling about how you must educate everyone and then they would understand.

"Understanding comes in the stomach," I said, turning the baby up for powder.

When I went out to put the baby to bed he ate the chop. Then he cleared the table so I wouldn't notice and washed all the dishes. I didn't say anything about it until later when I talked it over with Karl. "Why wouldn't he eat the chop?" I asked Karl.

"Damned if I know," Karl said.

"I guess it was too simple a way to do it," I said.

"If your belly's empty, it's empty," Karl said. "That's all there is to it to me."

"But it's different with him," I said. "It must be something more to him, something subtle."

"Well, the point is," Karl said, "he did eat the chop. He did actually eat the chop, that's the point."

"But he didn't say so."

"No, the say is worth something to that guy."

"Sure, the say is everything . . ."

"What the hell's the say worth? The point is he ate the chop," and Karl went off into a huge howl of laughter. I had to make him promise he wouldn't tell anyone so they wouldn't guy Hobbs about it.

"Yeah, he ate the chop," Karl howled.

Sometimes Hobbs would look like he had some mysterious grievance and wouldn't speak for days. He would come to the meetings or do some typing, but he wouldn't say a word and acted very polite and mysterious as if he had some great secret tragedy connected with him that he couldn't speak of. He would hardly speak to the boys, but he would come and take care of the babies while I did some work. It got awful hot and he would roll the babies out to the park.

He was always awfully clean. Once his collar was torn a little and he tried to mend it but he couldn't do anything with his hands. They didn't seem to have any life in them. We used to talk about it sometimes, how that fellow always had a clean shirt and his feet never stank. It's something to be able to do that when you never have a place to wash or a bed alone but he always looked scrubbed. I don't know how he did it, but no one ever asked him outright because he wouldn't have told anything, he would have had something mysterious to say, as if he had been washed in the blood of the lamb or something. Nothing natural and outright seemed to happen to him. Once I asked him if he ever had a woman.

"Didn't you ever have a woman?" I asked him because I couldn't imagine it, everything seemed so ideal and delicate to him. The boys always laughed at the way he came and sat with me like another woman. Once he helped me move and even if I did most of the work I felt delicate and precious. I had to laugh. The boys said, "Well, I suppose Sir Walter Raleigh helped you move." I had to laugh.

When I asked him if he ever had a woman, he blushed and spread out his long thin hands, "Well, if you mean have I ever been in love?"

"Well, all right, have you ever been in love?"

He looked at his hands a long time. I felt it as plain as your face that he was having a struggle between what had really happened when he was in love and what he wished to tell me had happened. I felt an awful disgust and pity for him, like shouting out at him, "Go on tell, tell me all the dirt, don't fix it up into the ideal, get it all out of your poor lean body, spit it out, vile and awful." But I knew he wouldn't tell me what had happened. There was something vague all over him. I saw the shanks of the poor guy, his shoes a little hard from being damp so much, turned up at the toes and hardened in the leather, living for the glorious mind and sitting, pawing webs over his own face.

He told me a long tale about his wife. I couldn't look at him at all. He said he had made five hundred dollars a month and had a pretty wife, and it seems she had fallen in love, he said, with a race track man, a driver of a fast car, and she had gone off with him, and then he said, and I was astonished, I couldn't believe it, that they had been killed, both of them, together. He seemed to like that almost and licked his thin lips over something. Yes, they had gone around the track together, driving very, very fast, he wasn't sure how fast, and they had both been killed.

About this time they were organizing a Hunger March to the state Capitol of all the farmers and unemployed to demand bread and milk for their children. Karl had been telling me that Hobbs never seemed to be there when anything actual was happening. He would talk or write plenty but somehow or other he never seemed to be at a meeting, where there was danger. I said to Karl, I couldn't believe it.

"That's the way it turns out," he said. "I don't believe it," I told him. "He's trying. He feels timid. He's sore from being alone."

"Just the same you'll see," Karl said. "Wait till the Hunger March and you'll see what I say is so, all right."

Before that we had a picnic down at the grove along the Mississippi. It was a fine summer afternoon in harvest, a good summer day with the wind blowing the heavy trees and the water like the sky and the little curl of beach golden in the bright sun. A day when you like to see your fat children running naked in the sun and water. Rose was there with her baby one month off and we all felt happy sitting on the beach with the tiny waves curling up and the sound of summer wind and the sun beating down into our pores like golden fire and the rosy naked children. Rose said, "Gee, I can't wait to see mine. I feel all the time like taking it out to look at it." Karl laughed and we all looked, laughing at each other through the sunlight.

Hobbs was sitting by himself and had taken off his awful shoes showing his long white toes but he wouldn't go in the water. We all put on our suits in the bushes and went into the river, but Hobbs wouldn't go in. He sat on the beach and that day somehow his eyes looked so cunning and dead I could hardly speak to him. And he somehow made Rose being so heavy with child seem out of place although we all liked it. "A woman," he said, "shouldn't come out like that." It made me kind of mad.

After we had lunch and Sybil and Karen were lying under a spotted beach tree sleeping with the shadows splotched on them, he said, "I don't see why people have children. We have no right to bring children into the world until we know more about it." Perpetuating the race, he called it. He got quite excited talking to me about it until I went to sleep too. I sort of dozed off, but I could hear Karl and Rose's husband talking very earnestly planning the Hunger March where they squatted down on their heels at the edge of the water as if they didn't quite have time to sit down even. Somehow the drone of their voices, earnest, real, coming through the heat and the wind, filled me with assurance. I wasn't afraid. The sun seemed to pour down on us expanding over and in and through the water and sky, sand and bodies and the lovely full mound of Rose sitting in the sand over her beautiful stomach.

"The masses won't stand together," Hobbs was saying, writing words with a stick in the sand. "They'll betray one another," he said. "They won't stick together . . . You can't make a silk purse out of a sow's ear."

I could hear the lovely drone of the men's voices and the life and dream singing in the heat, and our bodies intertwined together . . . "Look what the masses read . . ." I heard his dry voice going on and on.

A long time later I heard him say, "My wife and I might have had a child once but we got rid of it."

The afternoon of the Hunger March, Hobbs came over and stuck pretty close to me. He seemed silent and then he would talk very fast and loud. I kept thinking he would go but he helped me put on Karen's sun hat and said he would carry Sybil. It was a hot day but I was going to push the carriage up to the Capitol. I thought we could sit across in the park anyway and see what happened. The walks were sizzling, but Hobbs helped me push up the steepest hills. I was used to pushing them until I felt like a dray horse. We sat down on the grass on the mound across from the Capitol. We sat where we could see the marchers coming down University Avenue. The heat was like a falling curtain you couldn't look through. Hobbs had been telling me about a girl he saw at the Busy Bee cafeteria and what a pure face she had. It got to be past time for the marchers who were coming from the heart of the city. Hobbs got nervous and stopped talking and wrung his hands together in his lap. A dog lifted its leg right on the bench he was sitting on, but he didn't pay any attention. I let the children out of the buggy to play on the fine freshly mowed green grass. They don't get to see green grass too often.

Hobbs said, "What time is it?"

I said, "It's three o'clock."

After a while I said, "You keep yourself pretty safe all right." A slow color mounted his neck and half up his cheeks. He didn't say a word.

"Listen," I said, but then I could see the dark clot of men down the highway like a mass of angry bees moving swiftly towards the Capitol. "There they are," I cried, trying to see Karl, but they all looked like the same man, loose dirty clothes, angry pressing-forward faces, and all lean as a soup bone, but they came in a thick swift cloud, black and angry, bearing banners saying, *WE WANT BREAD. WE WANT MILK. OUR CHILDREN ARE HUNGRY.*

I began jumping up and down with a cry in my throat and my children climbing up my thighs. "Listen," I said. "You can still go. You can still join them ... Look ... Run ..." But he never moved.

He didn't come around for a long time after that. I felt sorry for the poor guy after all. I knew it hit him pretty hard, in a way, not being able to go that day.

We got kicked out of where we were living and moved into a kind of shack down the river. And one day there was Hobbs in the doorway making a bow, clean as ever, with his hair plastered down on his head as if he had been ducked in the river. He said that he had swum four miles down the river and walked back, but looking at him I thought he hadn't done it at all, that he had just wet his hair and then come up and told me a tale. It would be a daring, clean thing to do, to take off your clothes and go down a swift river . . .

Then he says that he got a boat for twelve dollars and that he expects to hear from his old advertising company in Detroit any day now and they will have a place for him in January, so he thinks he will go down the river alone for a spell and have an adventure until then. He sat very delicately in the room keeping his pants legs down so as not to show his bare shanks.

But, my lord, I even thought that maybe he would go down the river. A woman has always got faith and hope certainly. I felt glad and thought now maybe he will do it, maybe he will go down that river.

He sat on the couch telling about the books he had been reading. Pretty soon he got up and said he was going down to the river now and see about that scow he was dickering for and he stooped over and drew a diagram on the back of a leaflet, how he would fix it up for himself. It was all quite clear, there on paper.

Then he made a little bow, backed off into that space that would never protect him and went down to the river.

I didn't tell Karl anything about his having been there, but the very next day we got back from trying to get an extra quart of milk from the relief which they wouldn't give us, and we felt pretty discouraged because many that were demonstrating needed it worse than us and it didn't seem we got very far with all our organizing—and there was a note on the table, held down by the butcher knife stuck into it very dramatic, and scrawled on it with an elegant hand, it said:

AM GOING DOWN THE RIVER. SAVE ALL MY LETTERS. WILL WRITE MY ADVENTURES AND WE WILL PUBLISH THEM. IT WILL BE THE ONLY RECORD OF THE TRIP. SAVE ALL.

We never heard of him again.

The Girl

She was going the inland route because she had been
twice on the coast route. She asked three times at the
automobile club how far it was through the Tehachapi
Mountains, and she had the route marked on the map
in red pencil. The car was running like a T, the garage
man told her. All her dresses were back from the clean-
ers, and there remained only the lace collar to sew on
her black crepe so that they would be all ready when she
got to San Francisco. She had read up on the history of
the mountains and listed all the Indian tribes and marked
the route of the Friars from the Sacramento Valley.
She was glad now that Clara Robbins, the math teacher,
was not going with her. She liked to be alone, to have
everything just the way she wanted it, exactly.

There was nothing she wanted changed. It was a
remarkable pleasure to have everything just right, to get
into her neat fine-looking little roadster, start out in the
fine morning, with her map tucked into the seat, every
road marked. She was lucky too, how lucky she was. She
had her place secure at Central High, teaching history.
On September 18, she knew she would be coming back
to the same room, to teach the same course in history. It
was a great pleasure. Driving along, she could see her
lean face in the windshield. She couldn't help but think
that she had no double chin, and her pride rode in her,
a lean thing. She saw herself erect, a little caustic and

severe, and the neat turnover collar of her little blue suit. Her real lone self. This was what she wanted. Nothing messy. She had got herself up in the world. This was the first summer she had not taken a summer course, and she felt a little guilty; but she had had a good summer just being lazy, and now she was going to San Francisco to see her sister and would come back two days before school opened. She had thought in the spring that her skin was getting that papyrus look so many teachers had, and she had a little tired droop to her shoulders and was a little bit too thin. It was fine to be thin but not too thin. Now she looked better, brown, and she had got the habit of a little eye shadow, a little dry rouge, and just a touch of lipstick. It was really becoming.

Yes, everything was ideal.

But before long she was sorry she had come through the Tehachapi Mountains. Why hadn't someone told her they were like that? They did her in. Frightening. Mile after mile in the intense September heat, through fierce mountains of sand, and bare gleaming rock faces jutting sheer from the road. Her eyes burned, her throat was parched, and there was mile after mile of lonely road without a service station and not a soul passing. She wished, after all, that Miss Robbins had come with her. It would have been nice to be able to say, "What an interesting formation, Miss Robbins! We really should make sketches of it, so we could look up the geological facts when we get back." Everything would have seemed normal then.

She drove slowly through the hot yellow swells, around the firm curves; and the yellow light shone far off in the tawny valleys, where black mares, delicate haunched, grazed, flesh shining as the sun struck off them. The sun beat down like a golden body about to take form on the road ahead of her. She drove very slowly, and something began to loosen in her, and her eyes seemed to dilate and darken as she looked into the fold upon fold of earth flesh lying clear to the horizon. She saw she was not making what is called "good time." In fact, she was making very bad time.

She had been driving five hours. She looked at her wrist watch and decided she would stop, even if it was only eleven-thirty, and have lunch. So when she saw a little service station far down, tucked into the great folds of dun hills, she was glad. Her car crept closer circling out of sight of it and then circling back until her aching eyes could read the sign—Half Way Station—and she drew up to the side and stopped. Her skin felt as if it were shriveling on her bone. She saw a man—or was it a boy?—with a pack, standing by the gas pump probably waiting to catch a ride; she wouldn't pick him up, that was certain. These hills were certainly forsaken.

She went in at the door marked Ladies. The tiny cubicle comforted her. She opened her vanity case and took out some tissue, made little pads and put them over her eyes. But still all she could see was those terrifying great mounds of the earth and the sun thrusting down like arrows. What a ghastly country! Why hadn't someone told her? It was barbarous of the automobile club to let her come through this country. She couldn't think of one tribe of Indians.

She really felt a kind of fright and stayed there a long time, and then she got a fright for fear she had left her keys in the car and with that boy out there—she could see his sharp piercing glance out of his brown face—and she had to go pouncing all through her bag, and at last she found them, of all places, in her coin purse and she always put them into the breast pocket of her suit. She did think people were nuisances who had to go looking in all their pockets for keys. Habit was an excellent thing and saved nobody knew how much time.

But at last she drew a deep breath, opened the door onto the vast terrible bright needles of light, and there she saw through the heavy down-pouring curtain the boy still standing there exactly as he had been standing before, half leaning, looking from under his black brows. He looked like a dark stroke in the terrible light, and he seemed to be still looking at her. She fumbled the collar at her throat, brushed off the front of her skirt, and went into the lunchroom.

"My, it's certainly hot," she said to the thin man behind the counter. She felt strange hearing her voice issue from her.

"It is," said the proprietor, "but a little cooler in here." He was a thin shrewd man.

She sat down in the booth. "Yes," she said, and saw that the boy had followed her in and sat down on the stool at the lunch counter, but he seemed to still be looking at her. He looked as if he had been roasted, slowly turned on a spit until he seemed glowing, like phosphorus, as if the sun were in him, and his black eyes were a little bloodshot as if the whites had been burned, and his broad chest fell down easily to his hips as he ground out a cigarette with his heel. The thin man brought her a glass of water. "What will you have, ma'am?" he said with respect. "I'll have a lettuce sandwich," she said. "I'm afraid we ain't got any proper lettuce ma'am," he said bowing a little. "We can't get it fresh out here. We have peanut butter, sliced tongue . . ." "All right," she said quickly, "peanut butter and, well, a glass of beer." She felt that the boy was somehow laughing at her. She felt angry.

"This the first time you been in these parts?" called out the thin man from behind the counter. "Yes," she said, and her own voice sounded small to her. "It is." The boy at the counter turned his head, still with it lowered, so that his eyes looked up at her even though she was sitting down in the booth, and a soft charge went through her, frightening. She felt herself bridling, and she said in a loud cool voice, "This is a very interesting country. Do you know anything about the formation of these curious rocks that jut out of the hills? They are so bare and then suddenly this rock."

Was she imagining it only, that the boy seemed to smile and shifted his weight?

"No'm," said the thin man, drawing the beer, "I can't say I ever thought about it." She felt as if something passed between the two men, and it made her angry, as if they were subtly laughing at her. "I know it's hard to grow anything here, unless you got a deep well," he said.

"Oh, I can imagine," she sang out too loud; she felt her voice ringing like metal. The boy seemed not to be touched by what she was saying, but he attended curiously to every word, standing silent but alert like a horse standing at a fence waiting for something. So she began to tell the lunchroom proprietor the history of the country, and he seemed amazed but not impressed. It made her feel vindicated somehow. Still the boy drooped alert on the stool, his half face turned towards her, his huge burned ear springing from his head. She stayed half an hour and so cut her time still further, but she felt much better and thought she would make up for it. She got up and paid her bill. "I'll send you a book about the Indians," she said to the thin man.

He smiled, "That will be very nice," he said. "Thank you, I'm sure," and the two men looked at each other again, and she was amazed at the anger that gushed like a sudden fountain in her breast. She sailed out and got into the car. The thin man came after her. "Oh, by the way," he said, "the lad in there has had an awful time this morning catching a ride. He's got to get up to the bridge, about fifty miles." She felt they were putting something over on her. "I'll vouch for him," the thin man said. "He lives here, and I know his folks now for eighteen years. He's been to the harvest fields, and it would be something for him to ride with an educated lady like you," he added cunningly. The boy came out and was smiling at her now very eagerly. "Now they want something," she thought and was suddenly amazed to find out that she despised men and always had.

"I don't like to drive with a strange man," she said, stubborn.

"Oh, this boy is harmless," the thin man said, and that look passed between the two of them again. "I can vouch for him—good as gold his family is. I thought maybe anyhow you might give him a mite of education on the way." A pure glint of malice came into the thin man's eyes that frightened her. He hates me, too, she thought. Men like that hate women with brains.

"All right," she said, "get in."

"Get right in there," the thin man said. "It's only a piece."

The boy rose towards her, and she drew away, and he sat down in a great odor of milk and hay, right beside her, stifling. Without speaking she threw the car in, and they plunged up the bald brow of the hill and began to climb slowly. The sun was in the central sky, and the heat fell vertically. She wouldn't look at him and wished she could get out her handkerchief—such a nauseating odor of sweat and something like buttermilk. She couldn't help but be conscious of the side of his overall leg beside her and his big shoes, and she felt he never took his eyes off her, like some awful bird—and that curious little smile on his mouth as if he knew something about her that she didn't know herself. She knew without looking that he was bending his head towards her with that curious awful little glimmer of a smile.

He said in a soft cajoling voice, "It's pretty hot, and it's nice of you to take me. I had a hard time."

It disarmed her. She felt sorry for him, wanting to be helpful. She always wanted to help men, do something for them, and then really underneath she could hate them. "Oh," she said, "that was all right. You know one hates to pick up just anyone."

"Sure enough," he said. "I heard in Colorado a fellow got killed."

"Yes," she said, but she was on her guard. His words seemed to mean nothing to him. He was like the heat, in a drowse. "My, you must have been in the sun," she said.

"Yes," he said, "I've been as far as Kansas—looking for work."

"The conditions are pretty bad," she said.

"There ain't no work," he said simply.

"Oh," she said, "that's too bad," and felt awkward and inane. He seemed in such a sun-warmed ease, his legs stretching down. He had his coat in his arms and his shirt sleeves were torn off, showing his huge roasted arms. She could see the huge turn of the muscles of his arms, out of the corner of her eye.

They went climbing in gear up that naked mountain, and it began to affect her curiously. The earth seemed to turn on the bone rich and shining, the great mounds burning in the sun, the great golden body, hard and robust, and the sun striking hot and dazzling.

"These mountains," she began to tell him, "are thousands of years old."

"Yeah," he said looking at her sharply, "I'll bet." He lounged down beside her. "I'm sleepy," he said. "I slept on a bench in L. A. las' night." She felt he was moving slowly towards her as if about to touch her leg. She sat as far over as she could, but she felt him looking at her, taking something for granted.

"Yes," she said, "it would be an interesting study, these mountains."

He didn't answer and threw her into confusion. He lounged down, looking up at her. She drew her skirt sharply down over her leg. Something became very alert in her, and she could tell what he was doing without looking at him.

They didn't stop again. The country looked the same every minute. They rose on that vast naked curve into the blue blue sky, and dropped into the crevasse and rose again on the same curve. Lines and angles, and bare earth curves, tawny and rolling in the heat. She thought she was going a little mad and longed to see a tree or a house.

"I could go on to San Francisco with you," he said and she could feel her heart suddenly in her.

"Why would you do that?" she said drawing away, one hand at her throat.

"Why shouldn't I?" he said insolently. "It would be kind of nice for both of us," he was smiling that insolent knowing smile. She didn't know how to answer. If she took him seriously it would implicate her, and if she didn't it might also. "It would be kind of nice now, wouldn't it?" he said again with his curious soft impudence. "Wouldn't it?"

"Why, of course, I'm going to San Francisco anyway," she said evasively.

"Oh sure," he said, "I know that. But it isn't so hot going alone. And we get along, don't we?" He didn't move, but his voice drove into her.

"Why, I don't know," she said coldly, "I'm only taking you to the bridge."

He gave a little grunt and put his cap on his head, pulling the beak over his eyes which only concentrated his awful power. She pulled her blouse up over her shoulders. She had never noticed before that it fell so low in front. She felt terribly. And to her horror he went on talking to her softly.

"You wouldn't kid me, would you? You know I like you, I like you. You're pretty."

She couldn't say a word. She felt her throat beating. He was making love to her just as if she was any common slut. She felt her throat beating and swelling.

He kept on his soft drowsy talk, "The times is sure hard." His words seemed to be very tiny falling from the enormous glow of his presence, wonderful, as if he had been turned naked, roasted in the sun. You could smell his sunburnt flesh. And you could smell the earth turning on its spit under the mighty sun. If only he were not so near; the car threw them close together, and she tried to go easy around the curves so that his big body would not lounge down upon her like a mountain. She couldn't remember when she had been so close to a man. It was as frightening as some great earth cataclysm. She prided herself on knowing men. She was their equal in every way, she knew that.

If only she could see something familiar, then she could get back her normal feelings about men. She felt as if she were in a nightmare.

"I worked when I was twenty," he went on softly. "Made good money, blew it in on Saturday night. Made big money when I was twenty—Jesus, I've got something to look forward to, haven't I."

She sat over as far as she could. "Where did you work?" she managed to say. She prided herself on always getting information about people. They talked about Roosevelt and the New Deal. She always had strong views, but for the first time in her life she felt as if what she was saying was no good, like talking when some gigantic happening is silently going on. She didn't know what was happening, but she felt that every moment he won, was slowly overcoming her, and that her talk gave him a chance silently to overcome her. She was frightened as if they were about to crack up in a fearful accident. She relaxed on the seat, and the heat stroked down her body. She wished she wasn't driving a car. The great body of the earth seemed to touch her, and she began looking where the shadows were beginning to stroke down the sides of the mounds as if she might sleep there for a little while. An awful desire to sleep drugged her, as if she hadn't slept for years and years. She felt warm and furred and dangerously drugged.

It was as if a little rocket exploded in front of her face when he said, "Let's don't talk about that," and he leaned closer than he had. "Let's talk about you." She could see suddenly his whole face thrust to her, the gleaming strong teeth, the roasted young cheeks, and he had long single whiskers growing out like a mandarin. She laughed a little. "Who do you think I am?" she asked nervously. "Why, I guess you're a pretty good-looking girl," he said. "You look pretty good to me." She bridled at this common language, as if she were nothing but any girl you pick up anywhere.

"Why, I'm a schoolteacher," she cried.

He didn't seem surprised. "O.K.," he said, laughing into her face.

"Why, I could almost be your mother," she cried.

"Aw, that's a new one," he said, and he put his great hand straight on her arm. "Never heard of a girl wanting to make out she was old before."

She had an awful desire to make him say more; she was frightened. Swift thoughts, habitual thoughts, came into her head, and they seemed like frail things that the heat pounded down. Was it because they were so far out in these strange, rising, mounded hills?

"Are those cigarettes?" he said, pointing to the pocket beside her. "Let's stop and have a smoke."

"Oh, no," she cried, "I haven't time. I'm behind now. I've got to make up a lot of time."

"O.K.," he said. "We can smoke here."

"All right," she said, handing him the package. "You keep the package."

"All right," he said and took one out and put the package into his pocket.

The sun moved to her side and fell on her shoulder and breast and arm. It was as if all her blood sprang warm out of her. The sun moved slowly and fell along her whole side.

"Oh," he said, "I know you like me."

"How do you know?" she said offended, trying to see the road. She felt fatuous indulging in this adolescent conversation. She let her skirt slip up a little. She knew she had good legs, tapering down swiftly to her ankles. But he didn't seem actually to be looking at her; a heat came out of his great lax body and enveloped her. He seemed warmly to include her, close to himself.

"What kind of a wheel is that?" he said and put his large thick hand beside her own small one on the wheel. "Oh, it turns easy," he said. "I haven't driven a car since I left home. A good car is a pretty sweet thing," he said, and leaned over and began to fondle the gadgets on the front, and she looked fascinated at his huge wrist joint covered with golden hair bleached in the sun. She had to look and saw that his hair was black on his skull but also burnt around the edges. Looking at him she met his gaze and felt her face flush.

They fell down the valley, yellow as a dream. The hills lifted themselves out on the edge of the light. The great animal flesh jointed mountains wrought a craving in her. There was not a tree, not a growth, just the bare swelling rondures of the mountains, the yellow hot swells, as if they were lifting and being driven through an ossified torrent.

The Tehachapis rolled before them, with only their sharp primeval glint, warm and fierce. They didn't say anything about that in the books. She felt suddenly as if she had missed everything. She should say something more to her classes. Suppose she should say–The Tehachapi Mountains have warmed and bloomed for a thousand years. After all, why not? This was the true information.

She stopped the car. She turned and looked directly at him. "What is your name?" she asked.

Puzzled, he leaned towards her, that tender warm glint on his face. "Thom Beason," he said. The hot light seemed to fall around them like rain.

"Listen," he said gripping her hands, twisting them a little, "let's get out. Wouldn't it be swell to lie down over there in the hills. Look there's a shadow just over there. It's cool in those shadows if you dig down a little."

She saw his wrists, his giant breast, his knees, and behind him the tawny form and heat of the great earth woman, basking yellow and plump in the sun, her cliffs, her joints gleaming yellow rock, her ribs, her sides warm and full. The rocks that skirted the road glistened like bone, a sheer precipice and dazzle of rock, frightening and splendid, like the sheer precipice of his breast looming towards her so that she could feel the heat come from him and envelop her like fire, and she felt she was falling swiftly down the sides of him, and for the first time in her life she felt the sheer sides of her own body dropping swift and fleet down to her dreaming feet, and an ache, like lightning piercing stone, struck into her between the breasts.

She let her head fall over their hands and pulled back from him in hard resistance. She could not go to his breast that welcomed her. All my delicacy, my purity, she thought. He will not see me. I must not change. I must not change. The tears came to her eyes, and at the same time a canker of self-loathing, terrible, festered in her.

The moment had passed. He withdrew from her. "O.K.," he said. "You don't need to be scared. Only if you wanted to. O.K. Let's go. You can make up your time. We're only about a half-hour from the bridge where I blow."

She began driving very fast, very well. He withdrew completely from her, just waiting to get out. It hurt her, as if there had been before her some sumptuous feast she had been unable to partake of, the lush passional day, the wheaty boy, some wonderful, wonderful fruit.

"I'll swan," he said. "There's old Magill going with a load of melons. Hi!" he shouted.

She wished he was gone already. She wildly began thinking what she could say to him. She thought she would say, casually—Well, good luck. She felt easier knowing what she was going to say. She stopped the car. He got out and stood by the car. She wanted to do something for him. She really would have liked to give him something. She thought she would buy him a melon. "How much are they?" she said nodding towards the melons and hunting for her pocketbook. He ran over. "You pick out a good one," she called after him.

He came back with a large one with yellow crevasses. His strong talons curved around it, and he kept pressing it, leaving a dent which swelled out after his fingers. He held up the great melon with its half-moon partitions, grading golden towards the sun. She fumbled with her purse to pay for it, and suddenly she saw that he was holding it towards her, that he was giving it to her, and she was ashamed and held the quarter she had taken out, in her hand. He was smiling at her as if he felt sad for her. She smiled foolishly and sat pressing her wet hands together.

"Well, good-bye," he said. "And good luck."

"Good-bye," she said. Now she could not say good luck. He had beat her to it. Why should he wish her good luck when she had it?

He turned and ran towards the wagon, climbed in and did not look back. She drove around the curve, stopped, turned down the mirror and looked at her face. She felt like a stick and looked like a witch. Now she was safe–safe. She would never, never change, pure and inviolate forever; and she began to cry.

After five minutes she saw a car rounding the mountain to her right. It would pass her soon. She got out her whisk broom, brushed her suit, brushed off the seat where he had sat, opened the back window to air out the smell of buttermilk and hay, started the car and drove to San Francisco because that was where she was going.

Annunciation

For Rachel

Ever since I have known I was going to have a child I have kept writing things down on these little scraps of paper. There is something I want to say, something I want to make clear for myself and others. One lives all one's life in a sort of way, one is alive and that is about all that there is to say about it. Then something happens.

There is the pear tree I can see in the afternoons as I sit on this porch writing these notes. It stands for something. It has had something to do with what has happened to me. I sit here all afternoon in the autumn sun and then I begin to write something on this yellow paper; something seems to be going on like a buzzing, a flying and circling within me, and then I want to write it down in some way. I have never felt this way before, except when I was a girl and was first in love and wanted then to set things down on paper so that they would not be lost. It is something perhaps like a farmer who hears the swarming of a host of bees and goes out to catch them so that he will have honey. If he does not go out right away, they will go, and he will hear the buzzing growing more distant in the afternoon.

My sweater pocket is full of scraps of paper on which I have written. I sit here many afternoons while Karl is out looking for work, writing on pieces of paper, unfolding, reading what I have already written.

We have been here two weeks at Mrs. Mason's boarding house. The leaves are falling and there is a golden haze over everything. This is the fourth month for me and it is fall. A rich powerful haze comes down from the mountains over the city. In the afternoon I go out for a walk. There is a park just two blocks from here. Old men and tramps lie on the grass all day. It is hard to get work. Many people beside Karl are out of work. People are hungry just as I am hungry. People are ready to flower and they cannot. In the evenings we go there with a sack of old fruit we can get at the stand across the way quite cheap, bunches of grapes and old pears. At noon there is a hush in the air and at evening there are stirrings of wind coming from the sky, blowing in the fallen leaves, or perhaps there is a light rain, falling quickly on the walk. Early in the mornings the sun comes up hot in the sky and shines all day through the mist. It is strange, I notice all these things, the sun, the rain falling, the blowing of the wind. It is as if they had a meaning for me as the pear tree has come to have.

In front of Mrs. Mason's house there is a large magnolia tree with its blossoms yellow, hanging over the steps almost within reach. Its giant leaves are motionless and shining in the heat, occasionally as I am going down the steps towards the park one falls heavily on the walk.

This house is an old wooden one, that once was quite a mansion I imagine. There are glass chandeliers in the hall and fancy tile in the bathrooms. It was owned by the rich once and now the dispossessed live in it with the rats. We have a room three flights up. You go into the dark hallway and up the stairs. Broken settees and couches sit in the halls. About one o'clock the girls come downstairs to get their mail and sit on the front porch. The blinds go up in the old wooden house across the street. It is always quite hot at noon.

Next to our room lies a sick woman in what is really a kind of closet with no windows. As you pass you see her face on the pillow and a nauseating odor of sickness comes out the door. I haven't asked her what is the matter with her but everyone knows she is waiting for death. Somehow it is not easy to speak to her. No one comes to see her. She has been a housemaid all her life tending other people's children; now no one comes to see her. She gets up sometimes and drinks a little from the bottle of milk that is always sitting by her bed covered with flies.

Mrs. Mason, the landlady, is letting us stay although we have only paid a week's rent and have been here over a week without paying. But it is a bad season and we may be able to pay later. It is better perhaps for her than having an empty room. But I hate to go out and have to pass her door and I am always fearful of meeting her on the stairs. I go down as quietly as I can but it isn't easy, for the stairs creak frightfully.

The room we have on the top floor is a back room, opening out onto an old porch which seems to be actually tied to the wall of the house with bits of wire and rope. The floor of it slants downward to a rickety railing. There is a box perched on the railing that has geraniums in it. They are large, tough California geraniums. I guess nothing can kill them. I water them since I have been here and a terribly red flower has come. It is on this porch I am sitting. Just over the banisters stand the top branches of a pear tree.

Many afternonns I sit here. It has become a kind of alive place to me. The room is dark behind me, with only the huge walnut tree scraping against the one window over the kitchenette. If I go to the railing and look down I can see far below the back yard which has been made into a garden with two fruit trees and I can see where a path has gone in the summer between a small bed of flowers, now only dead stalks. The ground is bare under the walnut tree where little sun penetrates. There is a dog kennel by the round trunk but there doesn't ever seem to be a dog. An old wicker chair sits outdoors in rain or shine. A woman in an old wrapper comes out and sits there almost every afternoon. I don't know who she is, for I don't know anybody in this house, having to sneak downstairs as I do.

Karl says I am foolish to be afraid of the landlady. He comes home drunk and makes a lot of noise. He says she's lucky in these times to have anybody in her house, but I notice in the mornings he goes down the stairs quietly and often goes out the back way.

I'm alone all day so I sit on this rickety porch. Straight out from the rail so that I can almost touch it is the radiating frail top of the pear tree that has opened a door for me. If the pears were still hanging on it each would be alone and separate with a kind of bloom upon it. Such a bloom is upon me at this moment. Is it possible that everyone, Mrs. Mason who runs this boarding house, the woman next door, the girls downstairs, all in this dead wooden house have hung at one time, each separate in a mist and bloom upon some invisible tree? I wonder if it is so.

I am in luck to have this high porch to sit on and this

tree swaying before me through the long afternoons and the long nights. Before we came here, after the show broke up in S. F. we were in an old hotel, a foul-smelling place with a dirty chambermaid and an old cat in the halls, and night and day we could hear the radio going in the office. We had a room with a window looking across a narrow way into another room where a lean man stood in the mornings looking across, shaving his evil face. By leaning out and looking up I could see straight up the sides of the tall building and above the smoky sky.

Most of the time I was sick from the bad food we ate. Karl and I walked the streets looking for work. Sometimes I was too sick to go. Karl would come in and there would be no money at all. He would go out again to perhaps borrow something. I know many times he begged although we never spoke of it, but I could tell by the way he looked when he came back with a begged quarter. He went in with a man selling Mexican beans but he didn't make much. I lay on the bed bad days feeling sick and hungry, sick too with the stale odor of the foul walls. I would lie there a long time listening to the clang of the city outside. I would feel thick with this child. For some reason I remember that I would sing to myself and often became happy as if mesmerized there in the foul room. It must have been because of this child. Karl would come back perhaps with a little money and we would go out to a dairy lunch and there have food I could not relish. The first alleyway I must give it up with the people all looking at me.

Karl would be angry. He would walk on down the street so people wouldn't think he was with me. Once we walked until evening down by the docks. "Why don't you take something?" he kept saying. "Then you wouldn't throw up your food like that. Get rid of it. That's what everybody does nowdays. This isn't the time to have a child. Everything is rotten. We must change it." He kept on saying, "Get rid of it. Take something why don't you?" And he got angry when I didn't say anything but just walked along beside him. He shouted so loud at me that some stevedores loading a boat for L. A. laughed at us and began kidding us, thinking perhaps we were lovers having a quarrel.

Some time later, I don't know how long it was, for I hadn't any time except the nine months I was counting off, but one evening Karl sold enough Mexican jumping beans at a carnival to pay our fare, so we got on a river boat and went up the river to a delta town. There might be a better chance of a job. On this boat you can sit up all night if you have no money to buy a berth. We walked all evening along the deck and then when it got cold we went into the saloon because we had pawned our coats. Already at that time I had got the habit of carrying slips of paper around with me and writing on them, as I am doing now. I had a feeling then that something was happening to me of some kind of loveliness I would want to preserve in some way. Perhaps that was it. At any rate I was writing things down. Perhaps it had something to do with Karl wanting me all the time to take something. "Everybody does it," he kept telling me. "It's nothing, then it's all over." I stopped talking to him much. Everything I said only made him angry. So writing was a kind of conversation I carried on with myself and with the child.

Well, on the river boat that night after we had gone

into the saloon to get out of the cold, Karl went to sleep right away in a chair. But I couldn't sleep. I sat watching him. The only sound was the churning of the paddle wheel and the lap of the water. I had on then this sweater and the notes I wrote are still in the breast pocket. I would look up from writing and see Karl sleeping like a young boy.

"Tonight, the world into which you are coming"–then I was speaking to the invisible child–"is very strange and beautiful. That is, the natural world is beautiful. I don't know what you will think of man, but the dark glisten of vegetation and the blowing of the fertile land wind and the delicate strong step of the sea wind, these things are familiar to me and will be familiar to you. I hope you will be like these things. I hope you will glisten with the glisten of ancient life, the same beauty that is in a leaf or a wild rabbit, wild sweet beauty of limb and eye. I am going on a boat between dark shores, and the river and the sky are so quiet that I can hear the scurryings of tiny animals on the shores and their little breathings seem to be all around. I think of them, wild, carrying their young now, crouched in the dark underbrush with the fruit-scented land wind in their delicate nostrils, and they are looking out at the moon and the fast clouds. Silent, alive, they sit in the dark shadow of the greedy world. There is something wild about us too, something tender and wild about my having you as a child, about your crouching so secretly here. There is something very tender and wild about it. We, too, are at the mercy of many hunters. On this boat I act like the other human beings, for I do not show that I have you, but really I know we are as helpless, as wild, as at by as some tender wild animals who might be on the ship.

"I put my hand where you lie so silently. I hope you will come glistening with life power, with it shining upon you as upon the feathers of birds. I hope you will be a warrior and fierce for change, so all can live."

Karl woke at dawn and was angry with me for sitting there looking at him. Just to look at me makes him angry now. He took me out and made me walk along the deck although it was hardly light yet. I gave him the "willies" he said, looking at him like that. We walked round and round the decks and he kept talking to me in a low voice, trying to persuade me. It was hard for me to listen. My teeth were chattering with cold, but anyway I found it hard to listen to anyone talking, especially Karl. I remember I kept thinking to myself that a child should be made by machinery now, then there would be no fuss. I kept thinking of all the places I had been with this new child, traveling with the show from Tia Juana to S. F. In trains, over mountains, through deserts, in hotels and rooming houses, and myself in a trance of wonder. There wasn't a person I could have told it to, that I was going to have a child. I didn't want to be pitied. Night after night we played in the tent and the faces were all dust to me, but traveling, through the window the many vistas of the earth meant something— the bony skeleton of the mountains, like the skeleton of the world jutting through its flowery flesh. My child too would be made of bone. There were the fields of summer, the orchards fruiting, the berry fields and the pickers stooping, the oranges and the grapes. Then the city again in September and the many streets I walk looking for work, stopping secretly in doorways to feel beneath my coat.

It is better in this small town with the windy fall days and the sudden rain falling out of a sunny sky. I can't look for work anymore. Karl gets a little work washing dishes at a wienie place. I sit here on the porch as if in a deep sleep waiting for this unknown child. I keep hearing this far flight of strange birds going on in the mysterious air about me. This time has come without warning. How can it be explained? Everything is dead and closed, the world a stone, and then suddenly everything comes alive as it has for me, like an anemone on a rock, opening itself, disclosing itself, and the very stones themselves break open like bread. It has all got something to do with the pear tree too. It has come about some way as I have sat here with this child so many afternoons, with the pear tree murmuring in the air.

The pears are all gone from the tree but I imagine them hanging there, ripe curves within the many scimitar leaves, and within them many pears of the coming season. I feel like a pear. I hang secret within the curling leaves, just as the pear would be hanging on its tree. It seems possible to me that perhaps all people at some time feel this, round and full. You can tell by looking at most people that the world remains a stone to them and a closed door. I'm afraid it will become like that to me again. Perhaps after this child is born, then everything will harden and become small and mean again as it was before. Perhaps I would even have a hard time remembering this time at all and it wouldn't seem wonderful. That is why I would like to write it down.

How can it be explained? Suddenly many movements

are going on within me, many things are happening, there is an almost unbearable sense of sprouting, of bursting encasements, of moving kernels, expanding flesh. Perhaps it is such an activity that makes a field come alive with millions of sprouting shoots of corn or wheat. Perhaps it is something like that that makes a new world.

I have been sitting here and it seems as if the wooden houses around me had become husks that suddenly as I watched began to swarm with livening seed. The house across becomes a fermenting seed alive with its own movements. Everything seems to be moving along a curve of creation. The alley below and all the houses are to me like an orchard abloom, shaking and trembling, moving outward with shouting. The people coming and going seem to hang on the tree of life, each blossoming from himself. I am standing here looking at the blind windows of the house next door and suddenly the walls fall away, the doors open, and within I see a young girl making a bed from which she had just risen having dreamed of a young man who became her lover ... she stands before her looking glass in love with herself.

I see in another room a young man sleeping, his bare arm thrown over his head. I see a woman lying on a bed after her husband has left her. There is a child looking at me. An old woman sits rocking. A boy leans over a table reading a book. A woman who has been nursing a child comes out and hangs clothes on the line, her dress in front wet with milk. A young woman comes to an open door looking up and down the street waiting for her young husband. I get up early to see this young woman come to the door in a pink wrapper and wave to her husband. They have only been married a short time, she stands waving until he is out of sight and even then she stands smiling to herself, her hand upraised.

Why should I be excited? Why should I feel this excitement, seeing a woman waving to her young husband, or a woman who has been nursing a child, or a young man sleeping? Yet I am excited. The many houses have become like an orchard blooming soundlessly. The many people have become like fruits to me, the young girl in the room alone before her mirror, the young man sleeping, the mother, all are shaking with their inward blossoming, shaken by the windy blooming, moving along a future curve.

I do not want it all to go away from me. Now many doors are opening and shutting, light is falling upon darkness, closed places are opening, still things are now moving. But there will come a time when the doors will close again, the shouting will be gone, the sprouting and the movement and the wondrous opening out of everything will be gone. I will be only myself. I will come to look like the women in this house. I try to write it down on little slips of paper, trying to preserve this time for myself so that afterwards when everything is the same again I can remember what it all must have been like.

This is the spring there should be in the world, so I say to myself, "Lie in the sun with the child in your flesh shining like a jewel. Dream and sing, pagan, wise in your vitals. Stand still like a fat budding tree, like a stalk of corn athrob and aglisten in the heat. Lie like a mare panting with the dancing feet of colts against her sides. Sleep at night as the spring earth. Walk heavily as a wheat stalk at its full time bending towards the earth waiting for the reaper. Let your life swell downward so you become like a vase, a vessel. Let the unknown child knock and knock against you and rise like a dolphin within."

I look at myself in the mirror. My legs and head hardly make a difference, just a stem my legs. My hips are full and tight in back as if bracing themselves. I look like a pale and shining pomegranate, hard and tight, and my skin shines like crystal with the veins showing beneath blue and distended. Children are playing outside and girls are walking with young men along the walk. All that seems over for me. I am a pomegranate hanging from an invisible tree with the juice and movement of seed within my hard skin. I dress slowly. I hate the smell of clothes. I want to leave them off and just hang in the sun ripening . . . ripening.

It is hard to write it down so that it will mean anything. I've never heard anything about how a woman feels who is going to have a child, or about how a pear tree feels bearing its fruit. I would like to read these things many years from now, when I am barren and no longer trembling like this, when I get like the women in this house, or like the woman in the closed room, I can hear her breathing through the afternoon.

When Karl has no money he does not come back at night. I go out on the street walking to forget how hungry I am. This is an old town and along the streets are many old strong trees. Night leaves hang from them ready to fall, dark and swollen with their coming death. Trees, dark, separate, heavy with their down hanging leaves, cool surfaces hanging on the dark. I put my hand among the leaf sheaves. They strike with a cool surface, their glossy surfaces surprising me in the dark. I feel like a tree swirling upwards too, muscular sap alive, with rich surfaces hanging from me, flaring outward rocket-like and falling to my roots, a rich strong power in me to break through into a new life. And dark in me as I walk the streets of this decayed town are the buds of my child. I walk alone under the dark flaring trees. There are many houses with the lights shining out but you and I walk on the skirts of the lawns amidst the down pouring darkness. Houses are not for us. For us many kinds of hunger, for us a deep rebellion.

Trees come from a far seed walking the wind, my child too from a far seed blowing from last year's rich and revolutionary dead. My child budding secretly from far walking seed, budding secretly and dangerously in the night.

The woman has come out and sits in the rocker, reading, her fat legs crossed. She scratches herself, cleans her nails, picks her teeth. Across the alley lying flat on the ground is a garage. People are driving in and out. But up here it is very quiet and the movement of the pear tree is the only movement and I seem to hear its delicate sound of living as it moves upon itself silently, and outward and upward.

The leaves twirl and twirl all over the tree, the delicately curving tinkling leaves. They twirl and twirl on the tree and the tree moves far inward upon its stem, moves in an invisible wind, gently swaying. Far below straight down the vertical stem like a steam, black and strong into the ground, runs the trunk; and invisible, spiraling downward and outwards in powerful radiation, lie the roots. I can see it spiraling upwards from below, its stem straight, and from it, spiraling the branches

87

season by season, and from the spiraling branches moving out in quick motion, the forked stems, and from the stems twirling fragilely the tinier stems holding outward until they fall, the half curled pear leaves.

Far below lies the yard, lying flat and black beneath the body of the upshooting tree, for the pear tree from above looks as if it had been shot instantaneously from the ground, shot upward like a rocket to break in showers of leaves and fruits twirling and falling. Its movement looks quick, sudden and rocketing. My child when grown can be looked at in this way as if it suddenly existed ... but I know the slow time of making. The pear tree knows.

Far inside the vertical stem there must be a movement, a river of sap rising from below and radiating outward in many directions clear to the tips of the leaves. The leaves are the lips of the tree speaking in the wind or they move like many tongues. The fruit of the tree you can see has been a round speech, speaking in full tongue on the tree, hanging in ripe body, the fat curves hung within the small curves of the leaves. I imagine them there. The tree has shot up like a rocket, then stops in mid air and its leaves flow out gently and its fruit curves roundly and gently in a long slow curve. All is gentle on the pear tree after its strong upward shooting movement.

I sit here all the afternoon as if in its branches, midst the gentle and curving body of the tree. I have looked at it until it has become more familiar to me than Karl. It seems a strange thing that a tree might come to mean more to one than one's husband. It seems a shameful thing even. I am ashamed to think of it but it is so. I have sat here in the pale sun and the tree has spoken to me with its many tongued leaves, speaking through the afternoon of how to round a fruit. And I listen through the slow hours. I listen to the whisperings of the pear tree, speaking to me, speaking to me. How can I describe what is said by a pear tree? Karl did not speak to me so. No one spoke to me in any good speech.

There is a woman coming up the stairs, slowly. I can hear her breathing. I can hear her behind me at the screen door.

She came out and spoke to me. I know why she was looking at me so closely. "I hear you're going to have a child," she said. "It's too bad." She is the same color as the dead leaves in the park. Was she once alive too?

I am writing on a piece of wrapping paper now. It is about ten o'clock. Karl didn't come home and I had no supper. I walked through the streets with their heavy, heavy trees bending over the walks and the lights shining from the houses and over the river the mist rising.

Before I came into this room I went out and saw the pear tree standing motionless, its leaves curled in the dark, its radiating body falling darkly, like a stream far below into the earth.

Biography of My Daughter

For Rhoda

Listen, the biography of Rhoda is not very long. She was twenty-three when she died without knowing a lover and really only seven spring seasons, counting from when she was sixteen and wore a voile dress when she graduated from high school.

In the spring she and Marie came over to my house for lunch. It was one of the first spring days and we had fried rice and a green salad. Rhoda kept saying about my daughters, "They are so fat," she'd say in wonder. "Look, look at their feet, such strong, strong feet." She held their young fat feet in her hands, pressing the firm flesh. "I was born in a depression," Marie said. "I never had enough to eat."

We were all telling how we had been looking for work. Marie, who worked in textile since she was twelve, would get angry and her black eyes would blaze, but Rhoda seemed so gentle. You see lots of women like her and her mother, whom I saw later. They never say anything for themselves. They accept everything. They do their best. They believe in something. They live, they are silent, they die. Nothing is ever said for such people, no book is ever written about them, they never write a long biography saying I did this and that. Marie and I are not like that, a murderous anger smoulders in us, but there are millions of such people, lovely, accepting something too quietly. You see them sitting in a chair sewing lace on a garment, or looking for a moment out the window, and they seem grateful for too little.

Rhoda's mother was just like her, a frail gentle woman. She looked worn, just as Rhoda was beginning to look already, all the edges of her body worn away like an old machine. And after all, the body is not a machine, is it? They lived at a town called Starbuck and the father was a bookkeeper who was let out four years ago. After thirty years of hard labor he had scarcely anything to show for it except, as Rhoda said, "his girls." There were three other girls beside Rhoda. There was Rhoda herself, the oldest, and then Marilyn and Lucile and Bliss. You can see by the names something of what the mother expected of them. I expect the same of my daughters, somehow to be women whose bodies are not machines. Rhoda told about her mother that day, how quick and fine her hands were even in the middle of the night when she was sewing on some dresses. Later when I saw her at the sanitarium, I could see how her fingernails were worn down like a very fine precision machine that had been in use for a long time. She had a delicate and lovely face and all her girls looked exactly like her, only not worn down so much yet.

Rhoda sat in my chair that day. She was very quiet, her head drooping a little, and she read Mickey Mouse to my children and she listened to Marie and me talk. We were talking, I remember, with much anger and she listened even when she was reading, very tense, but withdrawn, as if it was too late for her to do anything, but she listened very intensely, and there was some frightful knowing in her. Once she stopped reading, and my two daughters, Rachel and Deborah, looked at her, and she said in a low voice, "When I was working at Mrs. Katz's I worked sixteen hours in a day... That's too long. That's too long."

I just got up and looked out the window and knocked over a pitcher of water, because I can't write this story. Rhoda has been buried two weeks now, and I really wrote this story tearing it out between my teeth when we were driving back from the sanitarium that morning when the corn was just ripening in the fields. You shouldn't break into a story like this, but it comes out like a burning behind my teeth, and that morning when she died, I could have swept down the fields with my arms, folded up the fields and crunched the city in my teeth.

I better go back carefully and tell about her. Perhaps Rhoda has a biography beside this one, too. You could find it on every relief record in Minneapolis, the city, federal and private relief. I saw her many times sitting there, her delicate blonde face and her body that seemed to droop a little from fatigue, and her disease, and she would answer all those questions politely over and over.

She came from Starbuck when she was sixteen to go to the university. She had to work her way through. She wanted to be a librarian. The first year she worked as a maid for only room and board, because her father paid the university fees, but the next year he couldn't pay them, so she got a job at Coffee Dan's and worked there as a waitress from six o'clock in the evening until two in the morning. From there she went to the Zaners, where she worked for her room and board. She got up at six, prepared breakfast, cleaned up, straightened the house and got to the university library school. Sometimes she got in some sleep in the rest room. She did this for four years. She was graduated. There was no library to work in. She worked as a maid, cook, waitress, then there was not even that. She was on relief. To get some kinds of relief you have to be examined by a doctor also. They found she had tuberculosis and needed a rest. Right after the day they were to see me, Marie went out with her to the sanitarium, and left her there.

She got worse. For two weeks she hadn't taken any nourishment. Marie and I started out in the morning to see her. It had been about a hundred for a week, the ripening corn was beginning to curl, but when we got to the sanitarium the green hills were rolling up to the summer sky where great white clouds hung still. It was about ten o'clock. "Gee, this is a swell place," Marie said. Some tubercular boys in shorts were playing ball on the green grass. We saw wing after wing of splendid brick buildings. "In a decent country," I said, "this would be swell, here it's a joke."

Marie looked saturnine and bitter, "For God's sake," she said, "look at it. What a farce! They wear you down and then they put you here and fix you up to wear you down again. Lookit," she said, "they should do with the workers like with horses, make glue out of 'em, when they wear 'em out. They should find some good use for blood, arteries, and bones in industry after they're no good as workers. Why bring 'em here?"

We walked on down the walk, Rachel and Deborah running ahead, excited by the palatial building and the fine stone steps. Marie suddenly whispered, the tears standing in her eyes, "I don't think she wants to live." We pressed our hands together. We looked up at the huge building. "Jesus Christ," Marie said, "how many well and living people this could house. Look at it, for God's sake!"

Rachel and Deborah ran back to us. "Listen," I said to them, "why don't you play out here on the nice grass?"

They looked up at the building. They had to tilt back their heads. "Listen, look," I said, "look how green the grass is." An anguish was in me like iron in my chest, "You can play tag here." They looked at the grass. They looked at me. They looked at Marie's dark and bitter face. "We want to go," Rachel said, snuggling up to my thigh like a colt. Deborah tipped back looking at the hundreds of windows. I saw Deborah and Rachel in the bright sun; their legs showed from the red dresses so fat, like conicals of flesh without bones. "Oh, stay in the green world awhile," I cried, and we tried to walk on, but Rachel gave a cry and wound herself about my legs. "What ... what!" I cried trying to push her away. "Listen, you don't want to go into that place." "Yes ... yes, take us in." "All right," I said angrily, pushing her away, and they flew up the stone steps, stopping at the door at the smell of death.

We went into the lobby. A man in white was brushing the floor. I thought we would see Rhoda like she had been in the spring, a little shy, putting up her falling gold hair, smiling at us, her head turned a little away. I saw a stone bench and picked up the children and sat them squarely on it. "You'll have to stay here until we see whether Rhoda can see you," I said. They sat there quietly while I walked away looking back at them. They sat close together, their eyes round, their fat legs hanging from the stone bench. I followed Marie down the corridor, into a room. I saw a nurse get up, come forward, I didn't hear what Marie said. I heard the nurse say, "Rhoda passed away this morning."

O daughter, what is child, daughter, then girl, then in voile with delicate hair?

Marie looked out the window as if she had not heard. I stood silently behind her. I felt someone behind me and turned to see a young girl with Rhoda's golden hair, a fuller mouth. Now her eyes were big and dark at the centers. Marie went to her and embraced her, "Marilyn," she said and began to cry. The girl stood looking around Marie's shoulder her eyes big and unblinking. "I can't cry," she said. "They woke me up and told me. I came out on the bus. I have to get back. I can't cry. I don't know what it is, I can't cry," she said. She was now working for her room and board at a Mrs. Katz's.

The nurse said, "Your mother is here . . ." In the door stood the mother plucking at her falling hair, just like Rhoda. Marie was crying. The mother patted her shoulder. She said to the nurse, "I've got all her things here." She held up a little bundle tied in a chemise. "I know Rhoda had pawned her things," the mother said, "but I can't find the little French book. Rhoda was very fond of that little French book." The nurse said quickly, relieved to have something that was needed for once, "I have it here, right here on my desk." "Oh," the mother said, relieved, as if something of vast importance had been settled. She put her hand on the French book and I saw her broken nails. She held up a pair of shorts. Marie cried out, "Those are the shorts I made for Rhoda." She took them. "I made them so she wouldn't be so hot lying there all the time. I made them," she cried looking amazed at them, as if it was strange that they should still be. "Oh, aren't they sweet?" Marilyn said, "too sweet ... " She had a deep lovely voice. And her eyes remained wide open as if she were walking in her sleep. "You have them, Marilyn," Marie said.

We stood there.

The mother said, "I guess, well ... I guess. . . ."

The nurse said, "You might as well go back to town. You can't get a train out of here for Starbuck until tomorrow at nine. You might as well go back to town and rest and I've looked everything up for you." She seemed eager as if she were relieved to be able to say that the trains ran on schedule, that everything could be done so well, so systematically. "Everything will be just fine now," she said. "Just fine."

We all stood there.

"What were the complications?" Marie said very low.

"Well," the nurse said, "I think her mother understands everything and that is all that is necessary."

A peculiar antagonism stood between us.

"Listen," Marie said, "I know what was the matter with her."

"Oh, do you?" the nurse said bitterly. "She had the best of care. I'm sure her mother agrees to that. The university doctor himself sat in on the consultation. Her mother knows that, I am sure. Her mother has already signed, saying she had the best of care."

We stood there as if she had not spoken. Marie looked strange. The nurse gasped as if she knew what was going to be said, as if an avalanche were coming slowly down upon the tiny room crushing us all.

Marie said, "She died of starvation. . ."

It was as if the flesh of each one of us shrank a little forever.

We stood there. The sunlight flashed back. The corn hung heavy on the stalks, the pumpkins and the squash were ripening in abundance.

"Now," the nurse shook herself a little, "you get your things. The train goes through here, right straight through here. We'll have everything arranged. . . . I've phoned Swinson already . . . she . . . she's in the ice room. Everything is all arranged . . . the . . . she . . . it will be put on the train you're on, everything will be just fine. . ."

"Thank you . . . thank you . . ." said the mother.

Child, then girl, with the delicate golden hair. The mother stood bewildered, holding the tiny bundle of Rhoda's clothes. It must have had just a brassiere, a slip, the dress she had come in, a brush and comb. "I can go back on the bus . . ." she said looking around, and I saw how she had never given birth to this. She had borne something, believed in something . . .

"You can go with us," I said to her. I knew her then. How she bore everything, said nothing, remembered four girls, had known their beauty, husked herself for their food, how she was part of the living and took what it gave, believing in something gentle, and now she saw death malignant and terrific. I ran ahead, into the lobby, and looking saw my daughters, sitting as I had left them, their feet dangling, their fat good and stout on their bones yet. I took their warm hands, ran out of the building. The sunlight fell on us, the green world reached up, engulfed us.

They came after, I could see the tiny figure of the

aging woman carrying that bundle down the walk as if asking a question. You give yourself over, with child, and see it blind at the breast, blind feet, blind hands. It sees then slowly, the moon, the stars, the sheep grazing, and grows up waiting for the good your body has promised it, and there it is dealt down like this. She didn't die of smallpox, diphtheria, measles, whooping cough, not even childbirth. She died of starvation.

The mother got in and set the thin bundle on her lap. To birth a child you carry heavy, heavy burdens, and death leaves a light burden indeed. Rachel and Deborah sat in the back close to her. I could see their eyes wide and big. We sat there, no one saying anything.

Marie was crying for her own death, for the blow that is dealt, for the thing that is and must not be.

We drove through the hills again, as if we were leaving an artificial world, something built up to hide a thing. "Listen," Marie said, "when she was graduated from the university I went to see her. There we sat and Coffman, the president, said we mustn't pay any attention he said to this shifting world, that's what he said. It's abstract science, that's what it is, go to the classics, he said, go to the good sane things of our forefathers, he said. Rhoda and I sat right there and heard him. We sat right there. Listen," she said, "she died of starvation. Listen, we've never had enough to eat."

"Easy," I said, "easy."

"Listen," she said, "say something for us, listen, say something. We've got to say something," she said.

We drove through the town past the morgue, *Swinson, Undertaker,* it said.

We stopped for some cigarettes. I could see the

mother's face dropping closer to the bone, gentle, gentle. I saw my children too solemn, real, waiting.

"My, that surely is a pretty place," the mother said, looking back. "They were real good to her."

"Oh, my God," Marie said, "on this fine summer morning . . . on this fine morning . . ."

Round pumpkins in the field, corn fattening, melons like the crescent moons of the season, hogs fattening on the hoof, this is the wheat corn belt, that is the rich, rich country.

"She went through college," her mother said in a weak voice. "She had her heart set on that. She went through college all right. She worked so hard."

"Look . . ." I said, "look, why did she want to go through college?"

"Oh, Rhoda was ambitious," she said. "Oh, she was a good scholar. My, I remember she always brought home the best report cards. We were always proud of her."

"Look," I said. I could see the city rising ahead of us, the university, the towers, the banks. I could have ground them in my teeth. "Look," I said, "I want to know. What did she want?"

"Oh, she worked so hard," she said, "she worked so hard."

"What for?" I cried. Her mother looked at me. My children looked at me.

"To be a success," she said at last. "She wanted above everything to be a success."

"It's a bitch," Marilyn said in a hard deep voice.

"Listen, listen," Marie said, "listen, she had it. Listen, this is funny. This is wonderful," Marie said and tenderness and fierceness were a brew in her that would make another world. "Listen, you know what she got? Four years she starved to go through that lousy place, you know what she got? This is a scream, two weeks in the library. Two weeks on the C.W.A. Hurrah! Isn't that something? Listen, after all that, two weeks as a librarian. A success! Two weeks work and a swell death. Listen, Marilyn," she says wildly, "listen, honey, listen darling, don't work too hard. If you get tired, you know what to do. Listen, Rhoda worked for a bitch, did all the washing, ironing, cooking, cleaning, eight people ... listen, honey, if you feel tired, listen, for God's sake, if you feel tired you know what to do ... there isn't any success. Listen, there isn't ... listen, if you feel tired, for God's sake, stop ... don't work. Stop, don't work ... work. Don't work your guts out. Listen, honey, stop ... don't work ... stop ... don't work ..."

Listen. Living I never thought of Rhoda as my daughter. She was not my daughter, but dead she becomes the daughter of all of us. She was not my daughter, but she might have been and my daughters may be lying dead like that.

What happened to her must stop happening.

This is for Rhoda. This is my daughter. She is dead but this must be a reminder of her to all people.

The Dead in Steel

For Anna and Amelia

Mother Anderson stood at the window, looking out on the street, waiting for the evening paper. In a few minutes her daughter's sons would come scrambling in and fill the tiny kitchen and bedroom to overflowing. The potatoes were cooking on the big range that heated the little room unbearably. She rubbed the dirty window with the palm of her hand to see better into the familiar street.

It was a day in March. The cold houses stood in water, and the winter soot fell from the chimneys. Old women, going to market picked their way around the puddles. A factory had been in this part of town and had moved away. Many workers had moved with the factory leaving the old black houses deserted. Now the spring sun shone and men stood on the corners with their collars turned up.

Such streets have a deep and sinister identity. The houses seem to bear sorrow like the bodies of women do. They are sad, mysterious and silent. To those who can read the lineaments of such houses, what life there is in them. They bend and sway and murmur their history like a tree–telling how a whole family have given their lives to buy it–the misery, poverty inside, the long years of anxiety so that the very wood seems dark and sad.

Mother Anderson looked at the street with the dusk settling like soot and she thought of her own dead, and the many dead she knew. When she was alone like this all the memory of her long life came back to her in short scenes so that it seemed they existed again and she could hear the lost voices speaking, of her husband, dead now for thirty years, killed in the mines, leaving her with eight children and one to be born. In the evening, especially in the spring, all this came back to her, all the burning days of labor, the many mouths to feed, the shack where they had lived in the teeth of the lake gales, the winter winds howling like wolves under the door, and the summer sun hot enough to boil eggs; all the great and burning legend of their lives, the years of toil, the bodies of her children now grown or lost, one son dead in a boxcar, one in the war, one daughter on the drouth-ridden plains of the Dakotas, one married to a barber out of a job, one now living with her with two sons to be raised by hook or crook. Now they would be coming home, the two sons and her daughters. They would bring the paper that would tell about the steel strike. The potatoes were boiling in the room and she turned to stir them thinking of all her babies, how nice they were, how clean she kept them, and Jon the best, the flower.

She hobbled over to the cupboard and took down a cup filled with money. It was the tax money, for the house in Milwaukee. To pay the ninety dollars a year taxes on it meant that they all had to do without, that Liza walked the two miles to work, and the children went without things they needed, but she wept to sell it now. Jon had put his money in it. They had all put their money in it, a dollar here, a dollar there. They built the frame first and for five years they could not finish the upstairs. After eight years, when Edith got her first job teaching they had put in the furnace and after that came the hardwood floors downstairs which made it fine. It was the fruit of all their living and they had all wanted a house of their own—but ninety dollars—she put it back and went to the window again.

The street was darkening now as if sinking into the rotten ground. She wondered if their house on Chestnut needed a new basement, probably not, because Jon had put in the basement himself before he died, and when he did anything it was done! Jon always knew how to do things. He was a builder. If only he hadn't gotten mixed up in the steel strike. And now they were at it again so she was afraid to look at the headlines in the paper. She thought it was all over in 1919, that she would never hear of it again and now they were at it again, in the Mahoning valley, in the Monongahela, names she remembered from Jon sending a postcard saying, Mama, we had a good meeting last night, everything looks good.

But she couldn't help but wait for the paper. What had happened? Those long dark nights in 1919 she had been out of her head for sure, out of her wits entirely, waiting to have word of him. It was worse than a war. He would call her in the night, she would hear his voice from God knows where, hoarse from talking, say—It's all right, Mama, we are all right. I'll be in Susquehanna tomorrow. We've got to organize more. Why did he have to do it when she sent him through high school and he could have been general manager of the brush works?

He used to come into the house and the other children thought he was crazy. He said it was like some people were yeast in the bread—Mama, you understand that?

And he went everywhere like for crazy, here, there, everywhere at once organizing men in steel. He would come in the middle of the night, tapping on the window –Mama! Mama!–she would take him in bed and warm him crying–Why are you doing it? Why are you doing it? He would say–Mama, don't worry your head, you will know some day. And he would go to sleep lying there, keen as a knife. What was he up to? Now after eighteen years, and him dead, other men were doing it.

She tried to see the towheads of her grandsons down the street. There, standing by the tailor shop she saw the short cropped towhead and skinny body of her youngest grandson, Jon. Jonny, he is too thin, she thought with a spasm in her heart like a fist inside her. He looked like her own Jon, the very picture, the spitting image, when he was a boy, and almost like a man working until the night to drag in firewood for his mama, always like a man and then out of his pants at both ends, long legs like a stork, what a time to keep up with it! He fit his father's suit except for the legs that the coffin covered. He was a mite longer than his father, went a mite further. Every generation must go further than the last or what's the use in it? A baker's son must bake better bread, a miner's son–each generation a mite further.

"Jonny, Jonny," she called, hobbling to the door. She saw him hear, but he didn't answer. She itched to get hold of him and she laughed softly in her mountainous ruined flesh so she had to sit down for a moment but she could still see him and hear his shrill voice and see him hopscotching through the junk yard, one leg caught in his hand in some rigamarole of his own.

He came to the door and was upon her, kissing her

old flesh, tickling her, resting on the firm bosom and the distorted stomach. His voice went in shrill cry and she laughed and made grunts and held him in her tree root hands, and half rocked and crooned to him and spat him on the buttocks sharply and he veered away crying, "Granny! You hit me too hard," and she said, "Be off with you," and spread out her skirts and tsk-tsked at him and wiped the sweat and tears from her old face, marked like a battle plain. "Hungry?" she asked, liking to feed anything. "Mmmmmmmmmm," the boy said wetting a finger to his ears by way of washing. "No," she shouted, sharp-eyed. "No, is that washing? Do you want I should wash you?" "Nooooooooo," he yelled, "Granny, I'm washing goooooooood." "Yes," she scoffed, stirring the potatoes, "potato pancakes don't go to any boy with dirt in his ears enough to grow corn." "Potato pancakes," he shouted and sprang to her again, putting his thin arms around her waist. She shooed him with her apron. "Go on! Go on!" she shouted and he squealed scuttering to the table and ducking under, sticking his nose in a funny paper he had hidden there. "What a nuisance," she mumbled, smiling, turning to the stove.

The older boy, Harold, came in like a riptide. He too, embraced her pushing his wild disordered face into her neck so she howled and pushed him, "I never saw the like of it. Out of my way. Have you got the paper?"

"No," he said, "I sold the last one, there wasn't nothing in it about the strike."

"So!" she said, "you wouldn't bring your old gramma a paper even. Have you got the paper money?" She looked into his huge ears that hung off his head.

"Ow!" he bawled, "Gramma, you're hurting."

"Hurting nothing, have you got the paper money?"

"Sure," he said, "what do you want it for?"

"You know," she said, shaking him by the ears. "You know well enough that today the taxes are due."

"No," he said. "What's the use of it, Gramma, we never see the darned house. I got it figured. We don't get much rent. We never see it way up there Maaaaamaaaa," he yowled seeing his mother come in the door.

She laid her packages on the table and turned on him like a cat. "What are you doing now?" she shouted.

"Doing!" the grandmother began.

"I ain't doin' nothin'," he said, "make her let go my ears, Maaamaaaa."

"Big Baby," she said giving him an amused whack. "It's the tax money I'll bet my bottom dollar. You don't want to give up your paper money."

"Naw," he said, "oh Mama ..." he stood in the low room ludicrous and long, his wild face in misery. He came almost to the low ceiling and his grandmother stooped, like a gnome, passing under his arms as she set the table.

"Don't say anything against that house," she muttered, "don't speak a word against it, my son. We all worked, I remember your uncles coming home every payday bringing me their money. Why, your Uncle Dan worked in a Chicago hotel and all he made was ten a week and every week he gave me seven, seven dollars!" She stopped wickedly waving a spoon at her grandson. "Seven!– he said 'take it, Mama, I get my board and room, a little for tobacco and my shirts'–and I says to him, I says, 'Dan, send your shirts home, I'll do them here, that will be fifty cents more,' and he did that very thing, yes sir, sent me his shirts mind you, every week, and I washed and ironed them and sent them back so he could wear them in that wicked city, Chicago."

"Mama, it's hard for the boys."

"Hard!" she said, "You don't know the meaning of hard. I had it hard."

"Yes, Mama," Liza said, "nobody had it hard as you."

"Mama, Mama," Jon said from under the table, "what is taxes?"

"He don't know what taxes is!"

"Oh, if I never heard of them myself!"

"Granny, what is they?"

"You got the education, Liza; what did I scrub out office buildings so long for to give you an education. You tell him what is taxes."

"Well," Liza said, "you have to pay them on a house, on property."

"Who gets it? Who do you pay it to?" His voice was a high whine of boys raised by women.

The grandmother turned an eye on her, "Who, after all?"

"The State. Well, it's the State," she said lamely, "you pay it to the State."

"Mammmmaaaa, what is the staaaate?"

"Why you know what the state is."

"Get up, get up," the grandmother said in a fury, flicking him with the towel. "Always under foot, like a cat I'll swear to God."

"Oh Mama, leave him be. He's got to read somewhere."

"Right under foot he always is, square under foot, slippery like a cat. Should I break mine leg on him?"

"Look, Mama, I got some celery."

"Celery!" they shouted. "Ohhhhhhmama, give, give me. I looove celery."

The grandmother gave them a cuff apiece, "Away! Are you pigs? I always raised my children good. No one ate till at the table and grace is asked on it." Jon began to torment her in a way she enjoyed and she swatted at him fiercely as he flew around her snatching at the celery leaves. "I can remember, my lad, when celery was something we never had." Harold turned on the radio so the women had to shout. They didn't seem to mind. It seemed to make a chaotic wonderful life in the room, the two women sitting knee to knee at the celery, the fair-haired boys trying to snatch the cleaned celery, receiving their playful slaps. Liza began to tell about things that had happened where she worked.

At last they sat down to table. Grace was said. It was dark now. Mother Anderson was thinking during grace that it was just this time of year that he had killed himself, this kind of early dusk, and she had been waiting for him to come home. She had said to him, "I'll have the house nice and warm when you come back. Don't linger with anyone." She got up and without thinking put a stick on the fire.

"Mama. Mama are you out of your mind? Here it is spring, we have no kerosene stove so you must keep the fire going! It will be so hot we won't be able to sleep."

"I'm sorry," she muttered twisting her apron around her hands.

"What's the matter, Mama?" the daughter put her arms around the strong sloping shoulders.

"Oh nothing," the old lady said, the boys were silent,

looking into their plates. The shrill sound came from the streets, the children playing.

"I was thinking of Jon . . ."

"Oh Mama, every spring . . ."

The boys stopped eating and looked into their plates.

"It was just like this. I said, 'Come back. I'll have the house nice and warm.'"

"I know it, Mama. Please, Mama. Look at the nice potato pancakes getting cold."

"Why should he have to be organizing steel? 'Mama,' he said, 'we don't live for ourselves alone.' Your Papa and I did. We always worked hard to get along, from dawn till dark we tried to take care of our own. That was enough for us. But him! Even me–even me he didn't care for like he cared for organizing steel."

"Look, Mama, please."

"You remember all that time he couldn't sleep he walked from room to room. That's one reason I don't want to sell the house, Jon."

"Yes, Gramma," he said, without looking up from his plate. They were so still as if the past, before they were born, had some meaning for them.

"Yes, I can see him walking around from room to room after the steel strike, that was in 1919, after the war. 'A few men can't do it, and you listen to me'–he would say, almost shaking me by the shoulders leaning over me with his burning eyes–'You listen to me, sometime there will be more and more and more.' The company he worked for before the war wanted him to be assistant manager. It was a brush company and he said, 'Mama, I can't do it,' and he sat right in the front room, remember, that room the way he had built it with a big window.

Jon made the plans out on paper himself. 'I know you'd be happy,' he said holding my hands, 'but I can't do it.' I said, 'Jon, be a district manager for me. Look, will it hurt you? Doesn't your Mama know what is good for you? Look, you can phone me from Detroit and say— Mama I can hear swell, I'm working hard to make my quota and I'll be district manager, and then we'll cele-brate. I'll bring you a silk dress from Buffalo, a hat from Milwaukee and shoes from Indianapolis and maybe a blue silk umbrella so you can make everyone jealous on Sunday. I'll even go to church with you and repent like you want me to . . .'" She dropped her hands on her lap, "He only laughed at me. 'I would like to do it for you, Mama,' he said, sad like, and then he said he was going down to the union hall. He was sick. That night you know what he did."

There was no stopping her now. They had all heard it before like a litany, a mass, a million times yet they sat as if in some deep sleep, as if they could not move. There was no stopping her now and they shook their heads like sleepers and looked at her.

"That night, the night before he did it he came and called at my door like a ghost so it gave me a start. I could feel my heart in my chest. 'Mama,' he said, 'come and sleep with me.' I got up and went to his room, that upper bedroom where his instruments were and his work-table with the drawings and pamphlets. He said, 'Mama, just lie down beside me, I can't sleep.' I laid down on the bed and I said, 'Tomorrow's the day to pay the taxes.' He didn't say anything and I said, 'Tomorrow's the day to pay the taxes,' and he said, 'Mama, don't think about it, what difference does it make?' I nearly jumped out of my skin. What? I screamed so—you remember, Liza—I told you about it afterwards."

"I remember, Mama," Liza said, "look, Mama, eat your pancakes."

"I thought it would quiet him and I started to make plans how we would improve the place; put in a basement, and hardwood floors in the dining room. And he got up and stood in the floor, shaking so I knew he had a fever. 'Mama,' he said, 'for God's sake, can't you think of anything else? Mama, for God's sake, be quiet. What is this house? They'll take it away from you. They'll bleed the life out of you. They'll squeeze you dry like a sponge!' I began to cry and he stroked my face and shoulders. 'Poor Mama!' he said, 'poor Mama! I wish I could give you what you want.' And the next day he did it. And it was the day to pay the taxes too."

Liza became excited as if her mother's fire awakened again the myth and legend of that happening, usually forgotten in the daily struggle, so difficult for her and so bitter; but now roused and heightened like an image in an old mirror so she saw again the happening, as if some myth was contained in it, and the boys raised their blue eyes in terror at their mother who suddenly became so lean and bitter, her hair loosened from the tight bun, warmth glimmering back into her bitten face so she was like a girl again, only more bitter and with something more vengeful in her. She spoke rapidly in good English, in a monotone that was more frightening than the naked flexible voice of the grandmother.

"I remember that day," she said, "the next morning. I always slept on the outside of the bed where I could rock the cradle."

"Was that me?" Jon said.

"Yes," she said, pinning him with her bright and fearful eye so everything in the room seemed, of a sudden, strange to him. "Yes, it was after I nearly gave my life for you to be born." And he was frightened. He never heard that before. Everything began to swim around him. "But this night my husband . . ."

"Was that my Papa?" Jon cried despite himself.

"Sh," she said, "yes, it was your Papa. He said, 'I'll sleep there, you sleep by the wall!' 'What has come over you?' I said. He never did things for me." Both boys hung their heads ashamed. "I slipped over and tried to go to sleep. But I didn't sleep very well. I always expected to hear the baby cry. Morning came early and my husband was bringing a cup of coffee to me."

"Unusual for him!" the grandmother said with a snort.

"Yes," Liza said her eye sharp as a needle. "'What is this?' I said. 'Let's dress early as we will be going early,' he said. I never grasped the meaning as I thought he was talking about the men who were hauling pulp wood through our land. 'Are they earlier today?' I said. 'No,' he said."

"Just like him," the grandmother muttered.

"'No,' he said, 'I mean you and I are going to Milwaukee.' And then I knew. I got cold all over. He said, 'Jon has done it.' I screamed and fell to the floor." She finished and looked at her sons and they returned her gaze unable to know how that could be.

"Bbbbut, Gggggramma," stuttered Harold. They always told the story this far and then they stopped. "Gggggramma, bbbut, you never say, you know what happened. Bbbbbut how did it happen?"

The grandmother laid down her fork, licked her fingers, looked at her two grandsons facing her. "He goes down and buys a little gun, a little gun for close shooting and he goes to the union hall that day I was telling of, to read, which he often is doing. And a man there named Lars says to him, 'Goin' to read?' 'Yes,' he says and he had a strong grin on him, meant nothing funny. And then he did it with the little gun."

Through the mouth, through the belly, through the temple, they thought. But they knew they had better not push the two women further, or a fury and a hell would be upon them.

"Jon, I'll tan your hide for you," his Mama said, "if you chew so loud."

"Mama, it's the celery makes the noise itself. Look I got my mouth shut right on it and it sounds like a snake."

Both women had to laugh and the two boys gauging their mood began to talk loud. "Look, it's spring," Harold said.

"I should know it," the grandmother said, "this is the day the taxes should be off."

"Mama, listen I got to have me a pair of skates."

"A pair of skates," mimicked the old lady, "he wants a pair of skates! It's millionaries we are for sure. Wouldn't you get me now a fine fur coat and an automobile?" she smoothed her stomach bitterly and turned down her great wound of mouth.

"Look, Mama, all the kids got skates."

"Yes, we're banker's spawn. Don't you know your Mama hasn't had a new dress?"

Harold went to his mother and hung himself over her

chair like a scarecrow. She stroked his arms with a queer smile on her.

The grandmother went into a fury which everyone enjoyed. "Look! Look!" she said rising on her weak legs which barely held the bloated and torn body upright. "I've worn this for ten years now. Look at it." She held up her mended skirts, "I don't know when I'll see something new. I don't for a fact. I'll wear it in my coffin. And there's the taxes!" she said, letting her ruined weight into the chair, "Jon always was telling me everytime he handed me the money, 'They'll take it away from you,' that's what he would say—'Mama, they'll take it away from you.'"

"Weeeellll," Harold stuttered, "well, I think he had ssssome sense, I dooooo. With that money we could have something good, we could."

The two women said, "Harold," together and he began to stroke his mother's arms.

"Yes," bitterly howled the grandmother, eating her cake with her strong root hands, "yes, what would I get me first? A stuffed davenport like a goose, for that corner of the room?" And she minced like a lady so the boys howled and threw themselves upon her. "A new dining set I should get me? A new silk dress and shoooooooos?" She screamed as they laughed and blew in her ears and searched for her lost ribs in the rolls of child-bearing flesh that hung on her.

Then a cry came from the street—*EXTRA-EXTRA.* She caught them to her as if a lion had entered the room. "Lord," she cried, "what is it now? A war? To take you from me. A war again. You can never tell what those mad men will do. Nothing do they know of borning a child. How many do they want to kill now so that not a woman's son walks the earth."

"Mama, it's nothing, probably just a murder."

She snorts, "Just a murder. Lord have mercy!"

The newsboy came down through the spring dusk shouting–*EXTRA–EXTRA–READ ALL ABOUT IT KILLEDINSTEEL KILLEDINSTEEL.*

The windows on the street were thrown open. Women leaned out. Men stood in the doors as if shy, not wanting to go out and meet whatever news the wild cry meant.

"Go. Go!" the old lady said. "Go find out. Don't stand there like jackasses. Like you are stone." She pushed two pennies into Jon's hand and he took off like a jack-in-the-box and in no time came running back, the white paper flapping in the dark.

"What is it, Mrs. Anderson?" A woman's frail voice asked out of the thick dark, full of cooking and the dim movement of men and women. They all stood in the doorway. The old lady spelled out the letters in the paper, the words forming on her mouth–*TEN KILLED IN STEEL.*

Liza was leaning out the window calling, "It's the steel," she cried, "men have been killed in steel strike."

"Go away," the old lady said sitting under the lamp, "go away!" and the words formed out of the page meaning to her the dark valley on the Mahoning and Monongahela, the long and dark valleys where men labored in steel.

"What is it? What does it mean?" the boys worried her skirts as she spelled it out, cursing now and then. "If it was only in my language, I could read it like a flash of lightning. Stop! Go away!"

Liza was talking to Mrs. Freed at the door. Men came out and stood together. Women leaned out of the windows hugging their arms together.

The grandmother at last dropped the paper to the floor and the two boys stuck their heads in it, the older reading like a low buzz of an insect.

"Mama! Mama!" Liza cried stricken by the quiet of the room seeing her two sons hunched on the floor, her mother sitting with a hand on each knee. "Mama," she cried again sharply, a fear striking her blood. Suppose she lost her mind? . . . "Mama . . ."

"Liza," she said, gripping her daughter in those strong terrible hands. "Liza, it's happened again. It's happening again . . . see, he was right. Jon was right! . . ."

Mrs. Freed came in, "Wasn't your son in the 1919 strike?" she said.

Liza said, "Yes, it was Jon, Jon was in it."

"I heard he was blacklisted . . ."

"Yes," the old lady said strongly, "yes, he was . . . he was. I tell you he said to me, 'You will understand sometime, Mama . . . yes . . . you will understand . . .' It's taken me eighteen years . . . now I know . . . it."

"Mama, what are you going to do?"

"Harold," she said, "Harold, get up from there. Mind what I say. Do it like I tell you! Here, sit . . ." She pushed back the dishes. "Write it down here . . . To the steel strikers . . . tomorrow put the money for the tax, put it in it . . ."

"Mama!" Liza cried and it seemed to her that they could not give up the house. All the great struggles, the thunderous, tumultuous history of the lives of nine of them seemed to rear in the room like some legendary beast; the cries, the tortures, the bitter laughter, the tender love seemed to be born in her brain and she put her hands on her mother's. "Mama, what are you doing, have you gone off your head?"

"Get out of my way ... get away ..."

"Mama, our house! ... Oh Mama, Jon's house! ..."

"No, it was never his house. A house for all, he said. And us like chickens, that's what, like chickens, scratching, fighting, yelling for ourselves alone. O, I am ashamed when I think of it. All those years, to think my children could get above all others. Now, it serves us right to be down, that we are with others ..."

"Mama, for Christ's sake ..."

"Gramma ... Gramma," Jon hopped around her. "Where is the money going?"

"We got something better to pay for. Write like I say it. Write clear. Show for what your schooling is good for. Show it now, write it clear! To the steel strikers and put this on it. For Jon Anderson—some will remember him ..."

"Oh Mama, you have gone crazy ..."

She looked out the window. Jon was right. All her living had not been lost now ... He was not dead. The only dead there are are the dead that do not have the future in them.

It seemed to her now nothing was lost, and the spring, the black air, the night seemed to rise like the plants, like something fertile in her, like tendrils from a horny tree. Suddenly the old dark and bitter street seemed to change, because she knew the dead now and other dead, like her husband, his lean and hungry face broken in pits. And from their hearts gnarled and heavy from the deep root of their bones, gnarled in the earth, there seemed to rise a fume of living.

Her old heart too, torn and twisted and deep and slowly beating all the days of her working–all the tortured births, all seemed to be for something. She rose up and walked to the window, looking out into the street through the geranium leaves. A strange rush of power surged through her body, through the broken, twisted and gnarled veins, through the great ropes and tangles of her blood. She saw the lean men together on the street. She saw her son lean as a wolf, tender as a deer, running, calling through the valleys of steel, through the fires and the darkness, and his mouth open and his hand to his mouth like a shepherd called in the old country, so they could be heard over the hills . . . The dead were walking again now, for the only dead are those who do not have the future in them.

"Mama! Mama . . ." she heard them crying behind her and she turned back to them.

Tonight Is Part of the Struggle

That afternoon she thought of the bright half-spring sunshine and people coming from the relief walking slow in the half cold half heat of March. In the afternoon so many men without jobs and the dirty snow on the ground. She had walked slowly along with the men and women, carrying Dave wrapped in a pink blanket and sometimes a woman stopped and lifted down the blanket and looked at the tiny head and said what is his name? She lowered her lids over her thin cheeks, I better not act proud because this is the depression, I haven't a right to have a baby that's what they say, so she would try to look like an old stick try to seem dry and brittle like old women, try to cover up her thin gold hair and make out like the baby bundle was a sack, some kind of old clothes maybe she had just gotten from the welfare and wrapped it up. But when she turned the corner and the sun blazed down as if lifting her, gee whiz, Jesus Christ it's baby and she felt the curve of new legs, the weak head falling against her, the pushing mouth ... but we can't give milk or cream or wheat you better nurse him as long as you can, it's the cheapest food anyway, it's a law now anyway you have to nurse your baby but with worry the milk goes and you have to be thinking at two o'clock, I've got to have milk, at six o'clock I've got to have milk, at six in the morning, at ten at two at six again I've got to have milk. Drink a lot of water, drink hot tea, that is good, Mrs. Ellgerty says, that is excellent.

If they only had somewhere to go at night, to get out of that awful room with the baby sleeping in a cracker box on the table and no place to go to get away from Jock and nowhere for him to go but out to get drunk if he could.

She had to go through an alley, through an old carriage arch that wasn't ever used now since the old mansion had become a boarding and rooming house and all the occupants on relief. She went up the dirty black alley and into the back door which led directly into their room. It must have been the kitchen of the mansion once. It was one room with a gas plate, a brass bed, one rocker and a table. Jock was sitting in his old socks reading the evening paper that he picked up from the next door before they got around to reading it. You couldn't get used to seeing him it gave you a start to see him home at four o'clock and you got mad seeing him sitting there ... for Christ's sake, Jock change the baby if you ain't got nothing better to do.

He saw her getting thinner, he saw her breasts, the peak of her dress wet from the watery milk. It made his guts ache. He threw down the paper, he spit on the floor.

She screamed. "Don't you dare spit on the floor when I broke my back cleaning it this morning." The baby started in her arms almost as if still in her. She laid it down as if she had been burned. She laid it on the table with the relief order.

"A fine Mrs. I have," Jock said, "can't get back in time."

"Go sit on your ass," she said and took off her terrible hat so her hair shot around her face. "I am pretty, I am pretty, Jesus, Jesus I am pretty. O Jock, look and see! I'm pretty as Joan Crawford . . ."

She had to get something to eat with him looking at her, hate screwing into her back.

He couldn't go into any room. There wasn't any other room.

Pretty soon he said, "It's snowing, Leah, it's snowing."

She looked at him.

"I see by the papers," he said, "there is going to be a mass meeting."

"A what?" she said.

"A circus, you nut, a mass meeting."

"You might talk as if I'm a lady," she said.

"Oh yeah?" he said, "parading all afternoon like any moll."

"Shut up," she said.

"Are you cooking prunes again, Jesus God, prunes, what do they think we are?"

"Listen," she said, sitting down to nurse the baby, holding out the big white globe of breast. Jesus, he thought, how can a little thing like that have such fine cow's breasts, for a kid, who'd have thought it.

"Listen," she said, "can't we go somewheres tonight? Every night is just like every other. A girl wants to have a little fun. I don't never have a bit of fun since the baby came."

"Sure, madam," he said, "Mrs. Rockefeller, I'll take you to the opera tonight being as how on account of I got a car-token that is just enough to get me down to the relief office tomorrow."

"Tonight is just like every other night," she said, "I got to get outen here. We might take a walk."

"We might take a walk," he said, "in the fine March wind, fine for the brat."

She laid the baby in the cracker box, letting his white fine head down easy off her thin arm. He let his arms wave as if signaling to someone not in the room. It was silent, outside the snow was falling. Somebody began to holler upstairs. She looked at Jock. He sat helpless looking at his hands. You could hear the sour sounds of people scurrying upstairs like lonely rats. The baby kept signaling. You could just see his hands over the side of the box. Outside the snow was falling as if speaking against the window, saying something.

"Do you suppose," Leah said, "that it is snowing everywhere?"

He looked at her, the things women said, how in hell should I know, am I supposed to know where it is snowing.

She began to cry softly as if she were alone in the room. It made him nervous. "Listen," he said, "why don't we go to that mass meeting at the auditorium?"

"I don't know what a mass meeting is," she said.

"Well, the auditorium is only one block away and it will be good and warm there and we'll see some people."

"Oh, will there be people there?" she stood up. "Oh, look look, Jock, I can wrap him right up, he won't wake up he won't even know and we can take turns carrying him."

"O.K.," he said, putting on his three-year-old coat.

"Listen," she said, "you wear the sweater under the coat, the wind is nippy."

"For Christ's sake shut up, put it on yourself."

While they wrapped up the baby, he mumbled on, "Put on the sweater yourself, that's what I say, that's the trouble with women always telling men what they ought to do, make saps out of 'em."

Outside in the dark alley the snow was falling softly and when they got out on the street being only one block from the auditorium, the hurrying people began to swell around them, caught them up in many powerful streamlets pouring into the main street towards the block-long building. The snow made a speed in the air, the people hurrying made another speed, men walking with women, bunches of men hunched over, blowing fiercely and darkly along in the wind together. Jock took her arm and she bent over the baby and they were caught up in a group entering the wide door with the wind blowing against them, all their bodies hunched the same way. They fell inside the building without the wind and as in a bas relief intent faces climbed swiftly up the ramp.

Jock said, "I was here once at a walkathon and it's nuts sitting downstairs, you gotta sit upstairs and then you can see downstairs."

Leah clutched the baby and climbed, it pulled her down in front to carry him. They came out on a giant shell a block long and they sat down on the side and already below was a vast ocean of dark people, and the sides of the shell were filling rapidly, people pouring in swift black rivulets.

They found a seat halfway down and she laid Dave on her knees. It was warm, people were all around them. "Jeez," Jock said, "this is going to be a lousy bum show."

"Shut up," Leah said, "it's warm anyhow, so many people make it warm anyway."

Men and women kept coming down the aisles, a heavy woman walked slowly. She was pregnant, her slow feet, searching only for food and shelter, broken on the flesh loom of childbed, at stove, at work. Below the dark clothes the veins were burst, erupted like the earth's skin, split by the terrible axe of birth. Leah shuddered. I will get like that. She shifted Dave so his feet dug into her empty stomach. "Sit still," Jock said, "do you want to go?"

A man was talking. She was afraid he would wake Dave but he slept without stirring, his head falling back a little and his mouth open. She didn't listen to the words very much, she looked at men's bodies, they always told her something.

"Listen," a man was saying, and she leaned back but his voice kept striking in every part of her. "Tonight is part of the struggle." He began to tell about things she knew about, how they were hungry, how they could not get jobs, how they must fight together. Jock looked at her and he also knew it was spoken to them. She leaned forward on Jock's shoulder to look at the man. He spoke in a very precise speech, was it Scandinavian, Finnish like her father who had been a carpenter, very gentle and precise speech. She couldn't see him very well, he must have been half a block away, but his voice coming out of the delicate shell of his body, and the words made her think of the iron range on the Mesaba where she was born.

"Who is he?" she asked and the man next her said, "That's Tiala."

"Tiala?" she said.

The man next her said, "It's snowing fierce outside now. Tiala is the district organizer for the Communist Party."

"Two years ago," he was saying, and the voice came large through the horns and now all the dark bodies were straining forward, "two years ago we had hunger marches, the seed we planted two years ago takes root now." He talked in terms of growing, of yeast in bread, she could understand yeast and seed, it excited her.

"The rank and file," he said, "the masses." She looked down on the great black sea of bodies, heads like black wheat growing in the same soil, the same wind. Something seemed to enter her and congeal. I am part, she wanted to say.

The voice was coming into them. You are producers, wealth is produced by hand and brain. I am a producer, she thought with her hand on the protruding belly of the baby, but not from hand and brain. She thought she was going to cry and Jock would kick her in the shins and yell at her when they got home. She heard only some of the words, the ones that her body's experience repeated to her, the class struggle, militant workers, the broad masses. They were like words in the first primer, gigantic, meaningless, but she leaned over with the others, to see, to hear, to touch, make real, make the lips form on them.

They no longer thought of going. Something seemed to have broken behind Jock's eyes, some hard thing and he looked frightened and open. It was like when you went home after a long hard trip. She wanted to cry down, "O Tiala, we are hungry, we are lonely, we are lonely and hungry. It's dark, and the snow is falling in March and the night is wide for Jock and me and we might get old without . . . O Tiala . . ."

No one could say a word. They all sat like a great black rock. Then suddenly the man on the platform seemed to ask a question and without warning the great body moved, hands lifted, mouths opened together and rising suddenly, lifted by storm and cataclysm, wind and the earth's eruption, the black body rose, lifted high, a black tide crest of hands, faces, shoulders, like erupted tree roots, black labor root erupted, rising black tide of labor bodies in a thick volcanic tide and there was a roar of flesh, roar of hands of a high key like a body of water on cliff sides, then, from man throat, from rocky Adam's apple, from chests deep with lifting, building, riveting there rose a terrible, a great manroar . . .

Aye. Aye. Aye.

The new flesh between her hands jerked as if lassoed, the breath caught in the thin ribs, the baby's face got red as when he was born, the nostrils shot open as if the noisy air was too much to breathe. At the last aye, it lifted its head, struggled and let out a bawl of rebellion, wonder, amazement and the young body cry topped the others, and faces turned seeing the pink blanket and there was a great laughter as they saw the tiny white head as Leah had lifted it from the choking and held it on her shoulder, the tiny white head like a dandelion top in spring sprouting there amongst the black froth of men from the tool and dye, carpenters' unions, truck drivers, tobacco workers, stockyard workers, and there the dandelion top new bright head as if just emerged and Leah hid her face behind Jock's shoulder and he wriggled trying to show it wasn't him and then he laughed and his ears were red and he put his big hand that was good on the Ford factory belt on the bright tiny head and his eyes said Leah, like when he wooed her.

The speaker was saying then, "... so Monday you must all be down to march to the capital to demand security for the workers. Bring your children ..."

She and Jock looked at each other. They had something to do now for Monday. She felt close packed with the others as if they were all running forward together. Outside the snow was falling in the heavy March darkness and the thick mass would move and spread, explode like black projectiles from their strength ...

And the speaker lifted his right hand straight up and he said in a loud precise and clear voice and she felt the strong taut thigh of Jock tensing next her and saw his knuckles white on his clenched fist ... "Listen," Tiala was saying, "fellow workers, remember, don't forget. Every hour, every night and tonight is part of the struggle."

"Farewell My Wife and Child and All My Friends"*

It was Monday, August 22, 1927. The morning came up out of the dark, hot and still as August mornings often are. Ruth woke and the sunlight seemed dark and spectral. Outside, leaning over the ramshackle balcony, the cherry tree was heavy under the dark sharp leaves, the cherries hanging together. How did it happen that the cherry tree survived, coming out of the rotten ground, amongst the tenements?

She reached over and touched lightly, with her finger tips, the warm breast of Tony beside her. He clenched his fist in his sleep and she saw the way his breast looked like a shield, divided by the black curls, setting sharp into the taut belly and the lean ribbons of thigh. His dark face on the pillow was like a dirk.

She heard Mrs. Clark moving in the next room. Why was she up so early? Surely they had kept it from her, she didn't guess that this was the day they would murder Sacco and Vanzetti. Hal, the organizer from the Sacramento Valley, was asleep on the couch but she could see only the rickety balcony and the cherry trees. She lay back softly on the pillow. If she lay on her side maybe the deep foreboding in her would ease. She looked at her

* Sacco's last words. Throughout the story the italics represent the exact words of Nicola Sacco and Bartolomeo Vanzetti, labor organizers executed on framed charges of murder, August 23, 1927.

body and counted on her fingers two months more for her. She couldn't stand the deep pain in her breast.

She got up and tiptoed to the kitchen and stacked up the dishes from the refreshments at the Sacco and Vanzetti meeting the night before. If there was no reprieve before nightfall, this would be the last meeting. She made sure there were six eggs for breakfast and then a fear came into her that the comrades had eaten all the bread last night, there were so many people to feed. No, there was that loaf she had hidden in the laundry bag.

She stood on the porch looking down into the dirty yard and the back stairs of a dozen tenements. She leaned over and picked a cherry. Without knowing it she began to cry.

O the blissing green of the wilderness and of the open land, O the blue vastness of the oceans, the fragrances of the flowers, and the sweetness of the fruits. The sky reflecting lakes, the singing torrents, the telling brooks. O the valleys, the hills, the awful Alps. O the mystic dawn, the roses of the aurora, the glory of the moon. O the sunset, the twilight, O the supreme ecstasies and mystery of the starry night, heavenly creature of the eternity.

Yes, yes, yes all this is real, actual but not to us, not to us who are chained . . .

She went back to bed and lay down, the cherries dropped on the balcony. She didn't want to wake Tony, he needn't know it was the day until later. All the noises seemed so tiny, the horses' hoofs on the street, the feet walking on the walk, two feet walking by sounded so lonely. She and Tony seemed tiny for a moment.

I remember when we youst live in South Stroughton,

9   Le Sueur Salute

Mass. in our littel sweet home and frequently in evening Rosina, Dante and I, we youst go see a friend about fifteen minute walk from my house and by way going to my friend house he always surpis me by aske me such hard question. So we ust remain there a few hour and when was about nine ocklock we youst going back home and Dante in that time of hour was always sleeping, so I youst bring him always in my arm away to home; sometime Rosina she youst halp me to carry him and in that same time she youst get Dante in her arm both us we youst give him warm kisses on is rosy face . . .

She got up and opened the drawer in her dresser. She took out a letter which wanted Tony to go to the Imperial Valley to help organize the lettuce workers. She looked around the room, then like a sleepwalker she got back into bed, watching Tony, eased herself down, put the letter slowly under the mattress.

She lay still listening. Mrs. Clark must have gone to sleep again. When she thought of Sacco and Vanzetti and how they would kill them, the bright sunlight seemed to turn inside out, to darken as in an eclipse. She didn't want Tony to get out of her sight. If she could hold him till the baby was born. She thought of all their times together, the way he told her about the old country, the way he first bought her a new dress, a white one with a colored sash, and the way she had never been lonely since she knew him.

Sacco had a wife and a boy and a girl. His wife, too, had to wake up this morning . . .

I remember a year ago on our love day when I bought the first a lovely blue suit for my dear Rosina and the dear remembrance is still rimane in my heart.

That was the first May nineteen twelve, the celebration day of the five martyrs of Chicago. So in morning I dress up with my new blue suit on and I went over to see my dear Rosina and when I was there I asked her father if he won't let Rosina come with me in city town to buy something and he said yes. So in about one ocklock we both went in city town and we went in big stor and bought a broun hat a white underdress a blue suit one pair broun stocking one pair broun shoes and after she was all dress up I wish you could see Rosina how nise she was look . . .

She propped her head on her elbow and looked at Tony's fine face, made for sun, made for vineyards, for the prairie . . .

Sixteen years since I left my fathers vineyard. Most of night I used rimaine near vineyard to sleep to watch the animal not to let coming near our vineyard. The little town of Torremaggiore it is not very far and I used go back and forth morning and night and bring my dear an poor mother two big basket full of vegetables and fruit and big bounch of flowers. Every morning before the sun shining used comes up and at night, I used put one quart of water on every plant of flowers and vegetables and the small fruit trees. While I was finishing my work the sun shining was just coming up and I used always jump upon well wall and look at the beatuy sun shining ane I do not know how long I used rimane there look at the enchanted scene of beautiful. If I was a poet probably I could describe the red rays of the loving sun shining and the bright blue sky and the perfume of my garden and flowers, the smell of the violet that comes from the vast verdant prairie, and the singing of the birds. So after all this enjoyment I used come back to my work singing I used full the basket of fruit and vegetables and bounch of flowers that I make a lovely bouquet and in the middle of the longest flowers I used always put one of lovely red rose and I used walk one mile away from our place to get one of them good red rose that I always hunting and love to find, the good red rose . . .

Tony flailed his arms, she put out her hand so he wouldn't strike her. He woke and looked at her. With a cry she turned to him.

"But if it's morning in Boston, then what is it here?"

"Well, it will be between nine and ten in Oakland then."

"It won't happen, shut up. They won't dare do it."

"Tony, what will happen?" She held the egg in her hand.

"How do I know," he said dowsing his face in water. "How does anybody know. God damn it, where's the towel?"

She was holding it for him. "Can they, will they like before, postpone it?"

"I don't know," he said, "nobody knows. I better wake up Hal. We got to be at the square in San Francisco by noon."

"Listen Tony, please . . ."

"No, I told you you can't go, honey. It's too near your time."

She wanted to be near him, she didn't even want him to go in the other room to wake up Hal. She wished they had some bacon with the eggs. They wouldn't have had the eggs only some comrade from Sacramento brought them up and said they were for the new baby.

Mrs. Clark came in, "Honey, I can't remember very well if the sun was shining, or if it was a gray day at Ludlow . . ."

"At Ludlow," Ruth said, not looking at her. "How many eggs can you eat, Mrs. Clark?" Everyone had to call her Mrs. Clark because she wanted to remember her husband who was killed at Ludlow. Now you had to be careful, sometimes great crevasses opened in her mind and then she saw the tents, the dead children, the women running at Ludlow. Sometimes this went away and she was a good worker, a splendid street speaker. She was a powerful stocky woman with red hair and a powerful chest, a regular bellows for lungs she had developed speaking outdoors. She could be heard a block in a pure strong voice. She had a broad strong Irish face and now she kept pushing her hair back from her face, and brushing her face as if cobwebs were in front of her. This was always a sign she was remembering again.

Ruth tried to be busy. Could she know what today was? They had tried to keep it from her. They were afraid for her strong fine mind.

"What time is it?" she said and Ruth thought she meant the execution.

"What time is it? It's eight o'clock, Mrs. Clark." And for a moment they heard the clock tick.

"What is it today?" she said, then sitting down by the table, her large white arms in front of her. "There's going to be something today, that meeting last night, for the life of me I can't think of it."

"Oh we are not going anywhere, not us. I think there's a meeting in S. F., the boys are going but you have to take care of me."

Mrs. Clark laughed, "Oh you, not you. You're strong as an ox. Why, before my first child was born I traveled all over Colorado speaking in mining towns, company thugs as thick as flies. What was that I asked you a while ago?"

"What time it was."

"Not that, something else, funny thing my mind..."

Hal and Tony came in. Hal washed. He was a strong blond Irishman full of laughter, a good organizer, and between the two men, so different, there was some strong bond that made Ruth jealous. She watched them as she put the toast on the table, everything seemed to be known between them as between lovers...

So in one lovely morning in September when the rays of sunshine are still warm in the soul of oppressed humanity, I was looking for a job around the city of Boston and away I was going towards South Boston, I met one of my most dear comrades, and just as soon as we saw each other we ran into the embrace of the other and we kissed each other on both sides of the cheeks. And yet it was not a very long time since we had seen each other, but this spontaneous affection it shows at all times in the heart of one who has reciprocal love and sublime faith and such a remembrance it will never disappear in the heart of the proletarian...

She listened to every word. She wouldn't leave the room for fear he would say something, perhaps he knew about Imperial Valley. She stood close behind Tony looking at Hal across the table, looking down at the lean head of her husband. They wolfed their food. They seemed to be always hungry. She always felt there was never enough to fill them. She was always fearful there wouldn't be enough.

Mrs. Clark looked at the two of them as if trying to remember something. They did not talk of Sacco and Vanzetti because of her, they talked about organizing the asparagus workers in the Sacramento Valley. But from the anxiety and sorrow in their eyes, the way they passed the toast to each other, she knew they tenderly salved each other's sore hearts.

Mrs. Clark looked out the window at the cherry tree, at the yard worn smooth by the bare feet of children.

"Listen, honey," Tony said reaching back and grasping her hands, "have I got a clean shirt, maybe a white shirt would be cooler."

She held his hand. She felt shy with Hal looking at her. "Come with me," she said pulling him. He looked at Hal as if he would have to humor her, you know why. She held his hand in the other room, "Listen, Tony, please..."

"No, for God's sake, you know yourself..."

"But what will we do? Mrs. Clark is going to have one of her days, what will we do waiting and waiting? We won't know anything, but what the papers say, we won't know a thing..."

"I'll send somebody back, honey. Listen," he said nosing into her neck softly, "darling, don't worry everything will be all right with me. I'll take care of myself, I'll send somebody back here, I'll send Murphy back, I promise, to tell what happens. I don't think the police will do anything, if the demonstration is large enough..."

"You be sure. You promise... cross your heart..."

"Yeah, sure for God's sake, honey, I know how you feel but you can't act like this..."

She felt ashamed and dropped his hand and stood still.

"Ready," Hal said from the balcony. "Some style having

cherries hanging right into your mouth here." He had hung a cluster on his lapel. Ruth laughed, the three of them stood close together laughing. Tony had his arm around her shoulder and Hal put his arm around her other shoulder and they stood in the morning sun of August laughing and he popped a cherry into her mouth. "Don't worry," he said tenderly, and they looked awkward and backed into the other room and got their caps. She ran after them. "Oh Tony," she thought about the letter. He turned back looking up the steps at her, laughing like such a boy and yet so strong like a weapon and Hal turning and saluting her from the walk, she felt all her fear gone and a strong pride came in her and she watched the two walk down the street without looking back.

At noon she left Mrs. Clark and went out on the hot street and looked at the headlines. *THAYER REFUSES PARDON. JUDGE REFUSES.* The streets looked unnatural, unreal. She felt a little sick so she went back to the hot flat. Mrs. Clark was lying on the bed. "Is that you, Ruth?" "Yes," she said and sat down in a chair as if in a tomb.

She thought of getting a ferry and going to San Francisco anyway but she sat on in the chair. She didn't know what to do. The clock from the kitchen ticked. Mrs. Clark came to the door her hair wild, looking strange as if she had been crying. "What is it?" she said, "I don't feel good," she passed her hands in front of her broad white face. These things leave a mark, Ruth thought, on every face, on every heart . . .

She had difficulty in breathing, the child, the heat, the terrible event seemed to press into her flesh on every side.

"Look, we'll have some lunch," she said. She looked in the icebox and saw an old meat ball sitting on a saucer. "There's some old lettuce Murphy got yesterday the market had thrown away, it's pretty good on the inside."

Mrs. Clark said, "We can have a salad."

"A salad would be good all right."

She started fixing a salad. Mrs. Clark kept looking at her. Margo, a young prostitute from above, came downstairs and asked if she could pick some cherries from their porch. "Ain't it awful, kid?" she said.

"Shhh . . ." Ruth said, rolling her eyes toward Mrs. Clark. They went out on the porch and whispered, pretending to pick cherries. "Today will they do anything?"

"I don't know, nobody knows what will happen."

"O the bastards . . . the law, the lousy bastards." And she said some more in a low even whisper, dropping cherries into the basket.

"Shhh," Ruth said, "let me know if you hear anything. I can't get out very good."

"O.K. I sure will. I certainly will. The bastards, that's the law for you, that's it, a shoemaker and a fish peddler, for Christ's sake. I seen it too. I know it. God knows, the lousy bastards . . ."

"Is it men she's swearing at?" Mrs. Clark said. "Does she think it's just men? Lie down, honey, take a rest. I'll wash the dishes, I'll clean up a bit. Lie down, take it easy, take a sleep, dream a good dream." Mrs. Clark put her arm around the girl. "You're sweet and the things you'll see, and the grand things the child will be seeing. Don't fret. Take a sleep, darling."

"That's it," Ruth said, "that's it, maybe we shouldn't be having a child. Maybe Tony will go away. Maybe no one should be having children nowadays what with everything happening like it's happening."

"Nonsense, stuff and nonsense," Mrs. Clark half shouted. She filled her great lungs with air, "Nonsense." She stood a moment, many things passing over her strong and lovely face. "It's the very time for it, of such blood as yours and Tony's. It's the very time to be having children, knowing how it is to fight . . ." She began to pace the floor talking in a rich flow of Irish memories with the great and wonderful histrionic power in her. Ruth listened to the legend of her life and the power and great fight in her and dozed off in the heat.

When she woke she was wringing wet and the clock had stopped and Mrs. Clark had stopped talking. Everything was very quiet. She washed her face and she didn't see Mrs. Clark anywhere. So she went down the steps into the street that seemed full of slow-moving people. There were fragments of talk along the street. ". . . It looks like they're gonna do it." The papers had big headlines, another extra, no reprieve. She went back quickly, past the old mansions now made into dirty tenements. She sat on the porch waiting for Murphy. Everyone who passed her stopped, leaning their packages on the railing and spoke of Sacco and Vanzetti in low moaning tones. She saw Murphy, a little bandy-legged Irishman, walking fast up the walk. He waved to her and grinned. "What a day," he said wiping his face on a bandanna.

"Murphy, what happened?"

"God almighty," he said. "There was a good meeting in front of the library, the pigeons walking around and mothers sitting by the fountains with their kids, we had some singing, everything was fair as you please when God almighty I never saw such a black sight, down from all the civil buildings, down the fine stone steps, from behind every pillar, God help us, vomited the black puke of the cops. They arrested some of our speakers, drove everyone out, even the pigeons God save us. Tony was safe so breathe easy and then the parade got going, fair to middlin' parade, and then the cunning cops with their fine wormlike brains managed to convoy the parade straight into the city jail and clapped shut the doors neat as a pin and there were our people, walked big as life into a trap and there they were in jail with the reporters looking for beards and not a beard amongst 'em, not a whisker, not a bolshevik hair. Hal was caught in the mess. Tony is supposed to speak over here tonight so he won't be home for supper. There's a heap to do and I got to get in touch with a lawyer . . ."

"Oh Murphy, thanks a lot."

He turned and hurried off on his bandy legs that covered the country twice yearly.

Ruth went upstairs and Mrs. Clark was sitting quite still in the kitchen. "We're going to a show," she said.

A breeze came up on the dirty hot streets, children sat on the curbs, women fanned on doorsteps. She kept looking for Tony. Every lean neck, gray cap . . . she kept looking for him. Mrs. Clark walked beside her with a big man's stride, her hands locked behind her back. She was silent.

Ruth went down side streets where there would be no papers. She was fearful an extra boy would cry out. The streets were dark and sad, men and women sitting silent on the stoops. "I'm looking for Tony," she said.

"He might be speaking on the street." Mrs. Clark walked beside her saying nothing. But it was early yet. The two women walked on down the street. Ruth looked at every clock. Five-thirty . . . six . . . They went to a little show down near the wharf. They had only thirty cents. The show was hot and full of men. A big clock shone in the darkness by the screen. Six-twenty. She could never remember what the picture was. Then the clock said seven. Mrs. Clark reached over and patted her shoulder and put her strong hand on her knee but kept looking at the picture.

Everyone seemed uneasy. Men kept looking back out the door. She got up and went to the door and looked out into the street. She could hear or see nothing. She went back. There was a constant stir in the stinking darkness. The clock now said eight o'clock. At eight-thirty she said, "I'm going, Mrs. Clark. You can stay."

"What time is it?" Mrs. Clark said, "Is it time yet?"

"For what?"

"Is it time they are going to kill Sacco and Vanzetti? Have they done it yet?"

The two women looked at each other. "You knew all the time?" Ruth said.

"Come on," Mrs. Clark said, "come on, darling," and she tenderly walked with the girl out of the hot darkness filled with restless men, out into the street. It was much cooler. Men walked up and down. The young prostitutes came down the black hot hallways and stood on the streets. They walked down to the corner where Tony usually spoke. Sure enough, there was a crowd that poured into the square, and Tony, his lean face lifted up, his body like a jackknife, leaning toward the men . . .

If it had not been for these things, I might have live
out my life talking at street corners to scorning men. I
might have die unmarked, unknown, a failure. Now we
are not a failure. This is our career and our triumph.
Never in our full life could we hope to do such work
for tolerance, for joostice, for man's understanding of
man as now we do by accident. Our words ... our lives
... our pains ... nothing! The taking of our lives–lives
of a good shoemaker and a poor fish peddler–all! That
last moment belong to us ... that agony is our triumph ...

Tony was saying in a clear voice, "They can kill the
bodies of Sacco and Vanzetti but they can't kill what
they stand for–the working class. It is bound to live.
As certainly as this system of things, this exploitation
of man by man will remain there will always be this
fight, today and always until . . ."

Children played around the black clot of listening men,
who looked like men perpetually in mourning, looking
up at Tony in his white shirt which she had ironed.

She edged up closer, skimming the edge of the pool of
men. Mrs. Clark came with her. Tony saw her and raised
his hand and she raised her hand and he smiled down on
her. The chairman took out his watch. There was a silence
as he held the tiny timepiece up. She couldn't think
anything was happening now, were they killing two men
in Massachusetts? She stood with her hand over the
kicking child.

The man put down the watch, there was silence. Tony
jumped down as another man began to speak and took
her elbow and they left the crowd, turned the corner into
a drug store. "You can have a soda," Tony said, "I got a
dime."

"Oh but . . ."

"Go on have a soda," he said.

"It's over," she said. "They've done it."

"Yes," he said. "Let's don't talk about it now."

"All right," she said and looked down at the table. The girl brought the soda. She looked at Tony and took his hand under the table. She turned one of the straws toward him and he took a drink. He gripped her hand. She was going to tell him now about the letter.

"Ruth," he said before she could begin, "I'm going to take Hal's place in the Sacramento Valley, until he gets out of the can, maybe longer."

"All right," she said. "I wanted to tell you there was a letter about going to the Imperial Valley."

"Yes, I know," he said. "The comrade from that district talked to me about it today but now I am going to the Sacramento Valley."

"I didn't give you the letter," she said.

"I know," he said, "that was bad, never mind. You'll be all right," he said in a low voice, leaning to her. "There'll be enough comrades to stay at the flat to pay the rent and the food, if you and Mrs. Clark do the cooking. Maybe I can even send you something." She knew he wouldn't be able to, probably not get enough to eat himself. She would send him boxes of food, maybe a chicken if she could get hold of one.

The extras were out on the street now. They heard the boys like locusts humming through the streets. "Extra . . . Extra . . ." They sat there holding hands.

"I've got to leave in twenty minutes," he said, "some comrades will be on the corner in a car . . ."

"Twenty minutes," she said. It was so bright in there.

He paid and they went out and down a block to a little dark park, full of fragrance of bush and flower. They stood back under a bush and he put his hands on her, made the lovely joke she knew about the child. There were men lying on the grass very silent, alone, and men sitting on the benches as if waiting.

"I won't go back to the corner with you," she said. "I'll be fine. I'll be all right."

"Don't hold out any letters on me again," he said. She put her arms around his neck and her hands on his smooth black head, "I'll be all right," she said.

When one loves another even in the torturous struggles as in poverty, the love rimains forever, here the love goes further, that is why we are still living and we will live in spite of the inquisitors and all that have sentence us to death because the world workers want us to be free and to come back into life, in the struggle for the love and the joy of liberty for all . . .

"I've got to beat it," he said and they stood close together for a minute and then he left her and she stood in the bush listening to his rapid steps down the walk.

Salute to Spring

For Mary Cotter

She turned off the squawking radio—the battery was running down—I want different news, I want to hear it, Lord, different news, she said out loud to herself as she went into the kitchen with the baby's bottle, thinking —her temperature seems better now and she wanted to hold the bottle herself—and seeing the landlocked, winter hills, snow-gripped, with the little black trees sticking out like the cross of our Lord.

The calendar above the stove said March, below a picture of a fat, naked baby. She reached up and tore the calendar down and tore the picture of the fat baby in two, and, as she poked up the fire, she threw the picture in.

Jim said, Why did you do that? She started. She knew he had been sitting in the corner of the kitchen watching the thaw on the land, wishing for seed. Why did he sit in the corner like an old woman speaking out at her from the cold darkness?

He watched her fix the bottle. She was such a tiny woman. At first her tininess had seemed strange and wonderful to him, but now it seemed ominous. He could see his children Michael and Ruth, far down the road between the black winter oaks coming home from school. They went only in the morning now. It would take them half an hour to come up the road, but he could see them lift and fall beneath the waves of the lower forty, which was already rearing up black out of the snow, clear on top and slopes. Another week, if the sun came out, it would be ready for seeding. Is she better? he asked, and he felt his voice awkward with guilt between them.

She didn't want to answer. I don't know, she said, taking the bottle out of the pan of water and squirting some milk from the nipple to see if it was too hot. She didn't want to talk to him. She resented his sitting there and he knew it. She went out of the room and he looked out the window.

She gave the sick baby the bottle and it suckled feebly, its eyes half open. She touched the open palm and the fingers curled around her finger. She had listened to the rasping breath night after night and now she was frightened by the quiet as the child looked at her from half closed eyes, voluptuously as if it did not have to fight now. Mary could see the hills out the window, her other children rising over the land and moving toward the house, toward food, toward her—the red cap of Michael rising on the wave crests and then disappearing as if he was drowning. She picked up the baby and held it as if those mounting wave crests were threatening, and she could feel the awful silence of the house, of the winter-locked land, that had gone on and on, day after day. The children would want food now when they got to the house and there was only the bread soaking in milk. The last of the store of potatoes had gone in last night's soup and Jim sitting in the kitchen like an idiot, in broad daylight, with no money to buy seed. A man got mad when seeding time was coming on and no seed.

She would find something, boil something; there would be something to eat. The child's head rolled back a little and the half open eye revealed the pupil as if looking at her and she began to rub the child as if she could put her own will back into it. She had a lean strong face; Welsh by birth, she had a strong will. She would do it; nothing would stop her; she had a will like the crack of a whip. What else could have kept her going the years since her marriage; three babies, carrying water, baking, milking cows, as if you had put a sparrow to doing all these colossal tasks, but you could see her running in the yard, even after dark, after the babies were in bed, looking for eggs, darting, running like a sparrow from nest to nest, looking under boards as if she could never stop, or never could know fatigue or despair, as if her thin, wiry bones were made of steel. She had such fat babies and she liked having them if only there was not so much work. She had a passion for her children, for having them, for giving them birth.

She rubbed the twig legs of the child, the thin chest, and held the tiny feet in one palm. She lifted one foot and put it to her mouth, put the cold toes in her mouth and blew on them. She leaned over and blew her breath on the child and she knew that despite everything the child had no resistance; it had not had enough to eat. She opened her shawl and laid the child inside close to her body. If she'll live till spring, she promised someone, it will be all right, there will be food, carrots, tomatoes; I'll plant them myself.

The children came into her house crying Mama, and that meant hunger. She put the baby back into the crib and the lips smiled curiously at her, as if the baby were very old, understood something.

She gave the children the dried bread and they seemed

silent and solemn as if they knew this was the last of the food. They ate, looking at their father in the corner until he got up, put on his coat, and went out.

Every move he made was like a knife cutting her. She felt him so keenly, shut in the house so long together, since harvest, his long thin body, his dark burnt face, both winter pallor and sunburn still on the neck and jowls. He was like a knife and every move cut her. Where you goin'? she cried out the door, and he went on down toward the barn. She threw her shawl over her head. The children watched her. She ran out after him, dogging his steps, crying, Where you goin', Jim? I'm goin' to town, he said back at her, walking fast to the barn and she after him, running to keep up with his scissor stride through the mud. Town, she cried, I'm goin' with you. She tugged at his coat. Naw, he said, ya better stay here lessen the baby needs ya.

She's better, she cried up at him; I got to get away from hereabouts. I got to get away too. He stopped by the pump and looked down at her where she stood in the wind, ready to fly at him like a black hen, her eyes snapping, her thin nervous body sharp standing against the wind, full of that energy and zip that always pleased him. He grinned at her. All right, he said, we'll stop and get Janey to come and stay with the kids. I aim to go right away now. She turned and ran through the wind into the house like a girl.

Jim had a hard time getting the old tin can started. They hadn't used it all winter and they had saved the four gallons of gas since September. She and the children stood at the window watching him crank. When it began to shake, she told Janey to remember the hot blankets for

10*

the baby, kissed the upturned faces of the children, and ran out. She saw the flattened faces of the children at the window, saw the children waving and she waved back until she and Jim were clear down to the turn.

It was wonderful to see other land, to get out of the landlocked landscape she saw from every window like a frozen sea. She knew Jim wouldn't say why he was going to town but she had read a letter, something about a meeting about seed loans at the fire hall, and she knew that must be where he was going, especially as they began to pass other farmers going to town. She knew everything he thought.He didn't have to tell her anything. She could feel his eye look at the land, calculate the seed, manure, lime needed. Fence posts down. She sat in her town hat and felt elegant to be driving to town. She didn't need much to feel wonderful. Life was brilliant in her and strong, and leaped up quickly in her blood for anything.

They drove through the lean strong hills she had known since her childhood, and Jim didn't say anything until finally he said, How we gonna live till spring? If he hadn't been driving he wouldn't have said this. How we gonna do it?

It was a relief; it was the first he had spoken to her about it.

Why, she cried, why, Jim, of course we'll live till spring. Why, what's got into you? Why, certainly we will, surely haven't we always? Is there ever a time when we haven't lived till spring?

Who's been complaining? I'm sure it's not me. Why, we'll do it; yes, sir. I aim to take those three sacks of wheat in the back seat old Dahl refused to take; I aim to get some money and a sack of meal and some credit this very day. I aim to get us something to eat all right. Why, it's a holy shame, a crying shame, crying to heaven, the way we been living in this town for years, had our younguns here, everything, and can't get more credit. It cries to high heaven; it does for a fact.

It's a hard time, he said.

A hard time, she cried. Ain't we always had hard times and those before us? Did ever anybody quit?

Quit having hard times?

She grinned, Well, if you want to put it that way. Hard times ain't quit and we ain't quit.

He felt better. He looked at her out of the side of his eye—that cute old hat she'd had on their honeymoon sitting on her head with the black hair combed straight back and her nose so delicate and sharp, by gad, she didn't look old. She was like a pullet settin' on a fence, by gad; she had spunk in her all right. He felt better and took out his tobacco and laughed.

Old lady, he said, you're full of vinegar all right.

Jim, she cried blushing, I told you—

He laughed and spit clean out the slit in the curtain.

The village street was full of men walking towards the fire hall. Yes, sir, she was right; that was what it was, a meeting on the seed loans which were due. She smiled and Jim looked away. They stopped in front of May's beer parlor and she got out and pulled down her old coat, looking to see who was in town. It looked like Saturday. Yes, sir, it was a meeting to see how they would get new seed. She saw Sadie Melthers across the street going into the grocery store. Jim said something that sounded like a grunt and went on down the street

11 Le Sueur Salute

trying not to look like he was going to the fire hall to the meeting, and she ran across the street.

The sun had come up and everyone was moving down the tiny main street in the sun. Puddles of water stood in the street where the snow was still melting. The big Moline plant was closed. No more engines running. The men were slowly meeting down at the fire hall, trying not to let their women folk follow. All the women were looking out of the windows of the stores seeing what their men were up to.

Mary talked to Sadie, whose children had been sick, and they both kept watching the men go down the street to the fire hall, and Mary went back into the store, looking at the canned goods, the flour, the fresh vegetables. She didn't ask for credit; she thought she would wait until after the meeting. She spoke to several women who were looking at the fresh vegetables but not buying any. Then she went out and walked down the street and went into the fire hall and sat down. There weren't many women there. They were afraid to come. All the men looked at her, and she felt afraid.

Ole Hanson was standing on the floor and he was saying, We got the bitter experience of everyday life; we taste it every day. We got to begin to know it. We got to begin to go forward.

He must have been talking a long while. Sweat stood on his lip and brow. He stopped and stood there and then slowly walked to his seat, wiping his horny head.

She sat leaning forward as if driving a horse that was running away. She heard everything they said, as one man after another got up to testify how he was willing and ready to pay the seed loans incurred during the long drouth, but that if he did so he would not be able to seed the land in the present spring. She heard them: losses of early lambs in the drouth, losses of pigs last year, no word of the bones that wintered in the lime pits. Feed none too plentiful. The men testified with the sweat standing out on them from the pressures of speech. Hard to talk now. A stenographer, a pretty girl from the city, was taking it all down when they said it. It was awkward putting down all the thick and heavy suffering into little words. The chairman said they knew that the pressure of collectors was not coming from the government who held the loans, that no one understood what was happening and that was why they were there today.

Yes, she nodded to what they said. She wouldn't have known she knew all this, but now it was said she recognized the words fitting the happening. Farrowing season this year much less favorable than last; death, heavy losses. Yes, she nodded, yes, yes.

A professor from the university got up to talk. He was a pale man with a tall head and what he was saying was very sad. She sat back against it. He seemed sad and his white head hung down on the stalk of his body. She looked at the men sitting around her like the scarred and ruined machinery that sat out in their farm yards. You know the way, she thought; they test seed corn to see how it will germinate. You can test a man like that too. Educated people, she thought, have poor generative power sometimes; they don't believe in anything. No good for tomorrow's seeding. No good to look to them; so she stopped listening to the professor. She didn't hear a word he said.

And then she blushed; the sweat stood out on her,

and she gripped her hands. It was Jim going forward, beginning to speak. He stood there looking at the floor. His hands hung down, a little longer than anything he could ever buy to cover them. The men all looked at him. It seemed a long time before he spoke. When he did, they were all startled. You could hear a car honk outside and the sound of the hoofs of horses, and the blacksmith in the next block shoeing.

What he said was, There's a noose around every man's throat. You can't see it this afternoon, but it's there just the same. No matter what we do there it is; we just wiggle around with the noose around our necks every single minute.

I believe in the Constitution, Jim said. I believe in America. She looked at him with new eyes. When he said that he believed in America the blood flushed into his face. He was a good speaker. You're a man, he said; you got the parts of a man; you got rights, you and your chilluns. We want to do what's right. We want to pay our debts. We always pay our debts. It ain't us who don't pay our debts, brothers. It ain't that we want to get away from the seed loans; that ain't the ticket, not by a long shot. No, sir. We can't pay, brothers. We can't pay. We taken the food right out our children's mouths to pay what we already paid, and that's a fact nobody can't get around.

There was clapping and the pleasure of the men at a quick tongue. Jim wiped his hands on his handkerchief and went on, If we pay our seed loans now, we got from seven years' drouth, we ain't goin' to be able to plant any wheat this spring. It's now planting time and nary a man's got seed to plant. And these here collectors it's got so you can't move the hay in your barn to feed a cow without uncovering a goldarn collector!

Men laughed and he continued, grinning, Yes, sir, you couldn't lift a bundle now without a collector popping out. It's getting worse, year in and year out; doggone, we all be put off like the rest been put off if we wait much longer. 1934 we had a crop failure. I cut 115 acres and put it into the silo and got a silo full of Russian thistles. During the fall I tried to get in on the feed loan and was refused and I was not able to get the waiver on the grounds I owed the bank. At that time I had fifty-seven head of cattle and I begged the federal reserve not to sue me, which he promised me to leave me alone. I said I hadn't beat anybody and both federal reserve bank and receiver of the bank were witness to my hand that they would leave me alone.

Now she understood it better. She knew now how hard this was for him to tell it. He had never even told it to her. She had not known what was happening. She had only seen it happening.

He went on slowly, One week later the sheriff served papers on me and in twenty days to appear before a court before them and judgment was added onto me. When feed loans came on I was not able to get waivers. I had to get along with twenty-five a month and I had to shoot thirteen pigs and in that winter I lost eight head of cattle. And during the spring or summer when the alfalfa came to growth I lost three horses. When we opened them after they was dead we found alfalfa clots in the belly. Now I got a girl that's powerful sick.

A pang went through Mary as if she had forgotten about the baby.

Now we got to do something. We got to begin to go forward. These things got to be known.

He stopped and stood still and she got panicky and tried to motion for him to sit beside her, and the chairman said, he thought they should appoint a committee to take what the secretary had put down and see that it got to the proper authorities so some action would be taken here, and he said, I appoint Mary, Jim's wife, because there ought to be a woman on this here committee to sit on it, and everyone was smiling at her and she felt all her own energy in her, the whole world, as if it was all in her, the energy, belief, wisdom. She got up. They saw a little black Welsh woman, her hat awry on her head, lean as a young pullet and strong in anger and passion.

I rise to say, I want to speak, she said, I think the women should be here because it is important the women be here. We know these things and we suffer because of them every day. What I mean is that we know it, and every year when we are still alive in spring, still for another year we are surprised. We are still alive for another year, we say to ourselves, and count our children, and every year we are just a little different with what has happened. Seven years now like in the Bible this has been going on. It isn't never over. It isn't never over. You say your children are an inch higher; you got one more—that's one thing we got no depression on; ain't no scarcity there! Alive yet; you are all alive! It's for hallelujah, sure enough. So that's what I rise to say. I never was on no committee, but I'll start being on one.

There was big applause. She sat down, surprised and happy. Ole Hanson got up and said that was a good speech and there ought to be more women there and he hoped they would be all together in unity, and go out of here with our arms around each other, and I hope half of us is women.

The fire hall cracked and split with laughter and the meeting was adjourned, and the pretty secretary ran down the aisle and put her hand on Mary's arm and said when would she come in and they could get the affidavits all together, and Mary looked at Jim and said tomorrow, and Jim nodded and took her arm and drew her close in to him and they walked out talking and smiling and nodding, with everyone excited and talking more than usual.

They got in the car and drove to the elevator. She put her hand on Jim's arm and said, I'm a-goin' this time. She got out and went into Mr. Dahl's office and said to him, I got three sacks of grain in the car, and I got to have something for my family. He said, I'm sorry but you can't sell it like that lessen you give one sack to the mill. All right, she said, you pay for two. Listen; you got to do it, hear? I got to have it and you got to do it elsen the committee will do something.

What committee is that? said Mr. Dahl. It's the seed loan committee, she said, big-like. Don't get excited, Mary, said Dahl. Mary said, Suppose you got four mouths to feed some supper and nothin' in the bin, nothin' on the shelves, nothin' in the cellar, nothin' anywhere. Well, he said, all right, I could do it, I reckon. All right, she said, do it. And he did.

They drove to the store and bought a sack of flour and she lost on the price of her wheat. She felt bitter and triumphant, and she said to Jim, Drive to the relief, I'm gonna get some hay too. He looked at her and drove to the relief. She went in and said to the girl there, Could we get a little bedding for our cattle? And the girl said they had all they could do to get straw to the animals. Mary said, Have you ever milked a cow? Why, no, the girl said. Well, then, Mary said, you don't know where the tits are on a cow. You know we could just as well wash our hands in manure, than wash the cow and that's the kind of milk that you and I are going to drink, I'm on the committee now, she said, and I want some straw for bedding. The girl said, All right, I'll do what I can. I'm a-comin' in tomorrow, Mary said, and I want it then. I'll be gettin' it tomorrow. I'm a-comin' in then to set on the committee.

And Mary marched out.

They drove rapidly into the frozen hills. It was supper and they had the supper in the back seat. Mary was feeling full of talk. They drove through the cold rise and fall of hills, the black thickets, and she felt herself full of energy of the finest kind. She wanted to sing, to shout, to say more words than would be heard like in the afternoon. What was the good of silence, each man sitting on his farm silent as a turtle? You see, she said– sitting close to Jim's long flank–it's never over. She felt like crying. More life, more life, break these awful deathly silences and suffering. We are strong, she wanted to shout. She pressed against him–we are strong. Nothing is compared to us. We are tough and strong. She began to laugh.

I swan, for God's sake, what's so funny? If you ain't the damnedest woman.

All those who are dead this winter–all those who fought in Spain, in China, all over the world, everybody who struggled, who said something . . . I read about a scientist and he kept a tick alive for seven years and put it on a dog and it hopped off to feed lively as all get out, hopped right off on the dog happy as could be.

He grinned, I'll be dogged, if you ain't the craziest–

A tick is nothing compared to us; it ain't a thing; it ain't got a thing on us; seven years' drouth, grasshoppers, this and that, one thing and another. That air tick ain't got a thing on us, not a thing.

I'll be dogged, he laughed. She could feel the air draw into his long, strong body. I'll be doggone, if it ain't the cats' whiskers. You would think of that. I'll be doggone if you ain't the sweetest craziest–and he slapped her thigh roundly and his big hand plundered her breasts.

Jim, you big fool, stop. What kind of goin's on in broad daylight on the road in plain sight? You'll run us plumb in the ditch! Jim, you almighty fool!

I'll swan, I got me some old woman, full of vinegar, full of what it takes. I'll be doggone.

She smiled. The dusk was blue and birds were flying in it.

They turned off the highway and when she saw the house she knew something was wrong. Drive faster, she said, and she could see the children at the cold windows and the girl in the doorway waiting. Her heart sank.

She was out of the car before it stopped, and she saw the baby in the crib still as death. She snatched it up and tried to warm it, blowing on the hands, into the mouth. Jim came in and took the child. Its weight was light as a sick chicken's, the eyes drawn back. You know when an animal is dying you can feel it. He gave her back to Mary and took the children out of the room. The baby seemed so light as if she were disappearing. The breath stopped, and a terrible wrench came from Mary as if she gave the child birth again, and she walked to the door and to the window as if she would call someone. The other children were hungry in the kitchen. It was dark and cold. She laid the body down and smoothed out the limbs, closing the half dreaming eyes. The tiny arms were not made for crossing.

She went into the kitchen, got supper, and they ate it.

She put the children to bed. Jim went out to do the chores. The children were wide-eyed in bed and she lay down beside them to soothe their fright. She wanted to say something as if an upsurge of words lay buried beneath her skin. She could see the baby's head in the crib, disappearing in the deepening dusk. It seemed quiet now where it had been—no more fretting and fever and hunger.

The children sighed and murmured and touched her and went to sleep. She waited for Jim to come back into the house. She put out her hand and felt the legs of Michael, willful like his father, and the soft fair skull of Ruth. Spring and children's voices again.

She must have slept. The house was quiet; the dog walked softly in the kitchen. The honk of the ducks sounded far into the sky. She heard Jim approach the house, come in at the door. She saw him light the lamp and turn it low and look at the dead child. He covered her with an old coat and the light went out and she heard him get into bed.

She got up. She went past the dead child in the crib. No need to ever cover her now.

She got into bed beside him. He turned the strong scythe of his legs, the thrust and cleft of breast, and she turned into him, crying.

I Was Marching

Minneapolis, 1934

I have never been in a strike before. It is like looking at something that is happening for the first time and there are no thoughts and no words yet accrued to it. If you come from the middle class, words are likely to mean more than an event. You are likely to think about a thing, and the happening will be the size of a pin-point and the words around the happening very large, distorting it queerly. It's a case of "Remembrance of Things Past." When you are in the event, you are likely to have a distinctly individualistic attitude, to be only partly there, and to care more for the happening afterwards than when it is happening. That is why it is hard for a person like myself and others to be in a strike.

Besides, in American life, you hear things happening in a far and muffled way. One thing is said and another happens. Our merchant society has been built upon a huge hypocrisy, a cutthroat competition which sets one man against another and at the same time an ideology mouthing such words as "Humanity," "Truth," the "Golden Rule," and such. Now in a crisis the word falls away and the skeleton of that action shows in terrific movement.

For two days I heard of the strike. I went by their headquarters, I walked by on the opposite side of the street and saw the dark old building that had been a garage and lean, dark young faces leaning from the upstairs windows. I had to go down there often. I looked in. I saw the huge black interior and live coals of living men moving restlessly and orderly, their eyes gleaming from their sweaty faces.

I saw cars leaving filled with grimy men, pickets going to the line, engines roaring out. I stayed close to the door, watching. I didn't go in. I was afraid they would put me out. After all, I could remain a spectator. A man wearing a polo hat kept going around with a large camera taking pictures.

I am putting down exactly how I felt, because I believe others of my class feel the same as I did. I believe it stands for an important psychic change that must take place in all. I saw many artists, writers, professionals, even businessmen and women standing across the street, too, and I saw in their faces the same longings, the same fears.

The truth is I was afraid. Not of the physical danger at all, but an awful fright of mixing, of losing myself, of being unknown and lost. I felt inferior. I felt no one would know me there, that all I had been trained to excel in would go unnoticed. I can't describe what I felt, but perhaps it will come near it to say that I felt I excelled in competing with others and I knew instantly that these people were not competing at all, that they were acting in a strange, powerful trance of movement together. And I was filled with longing to act with them and with fear that I could not. I felt I was born out of every kind of life, thrown up alone, looking at other lonely people, a condition I had been in the habit of defending with various attitudes of cynicism, preciosity, defiance, and hatred.

Looking at that dark and lively building, massed with men, I knew my feelings to be those belonging to disruption, chaos, and disintegration and I felt their direct and awful movement, mute and powerful, drawing them into a close and glowing cohesion like a powerful conflagration in the midst of the city. And it filled me with fear and awe and at the same time hope. I knew this action to be prophetic and indicative of future actions and I wanted to be part of it.

Our life seems to be marked with a curious and muffled violence over America, but this action has always been in the dark, men and women dying obscurely, poor and poverty marked lives, but now from city to city runs this violence, into the open, and colossal happenings stand bare before our eyes, the street churning suddenly upon the pivot of mad violence, whole men suddenly spouting blood and running like living sieves, another holding a dangling arm shot squarely off, a tall youngster, running, tripping over his intestines, and one block away, in the burning sun, gay women shopping and a window dresser trying to decide whether to put green or red voile on a manikin.

In these terrible happenings you cannot be neutral now. No one can be neutral in the face of bullets.

The next day, with sweat breaking out on my body, I walked past the three guards at the door. They said, "Let the women in. We need women." And I knew it was no joke.

At first I could not see into the dark building. I felt many men coming and going, cars driving through. I had an awful impulse to go into the office which I passed, and offer to do some special work. I saw a sign which said, "Get your button." I saw they all had buttons with the date and the number of the union local. I didn't get a button. I wanted to be anonymous.

There seemed to be a current, running down the wooden stairs, towards the front of the building, into the street, that was massed with people, and back again. I followed the current up the old stairs packed closely with hot men and women. As I was going up I could look down and see the lower floor, the cars drawing up to await picket call, the hospital roped off on one side.

Upstairs men sat bolt upright in chairs asleep, their bodies flung in attitudes of peculiar violence of fatigue. A woman nursed her baby. Two young girls slept together on a cot, dressed in overalls. The voice of the loudspeaker filled the room. The immense heat pressed down from the flat ceiling. I stood up against the wall for an hour. No one paid any attention to me. The commissary was in back and the women came out sometimes and sat down, fanning themselves with their aprons and listening to the news over the loudspeaker. A huge man seemed hung on a tiny folding chair. Occasionally someone tiptoed over and brushed the flies off his face. His great head fell over and the sweat poured regularly from his forehead like a spring. I wondered why they took such care of him. They all looked at him tenderly as he slept. I learned later he was a leader on the picket line and had the scalps of more cops to his name than any other.

Three windows flanked the front. I walked over to the windows. A red-headed woman with a button saying, "Unemployed Council," was looking out. I looked out with her. A thick crowd stood in the heat below listening to the strike bulletin. We could look right into the windows of the smart club across the street. We could see people peering out of the windows half hidden.

I kept feeling they would put me out. No one paid any attention. The woman said without looking at me, nodding to the palatial house, "It sure is good to see the enemy plain like that." "Yes," I said. I saw that the club was surrounded by a steel picket fence higher than a man. "They know what they put that there fence there for," she said. "Yes," I said. "Well," she said, "I've got to get back to the kitchen. Is it ever hot?" The thermometer said ninety-nine. The sweat ran off us, burning our skins. "The boys'll be coming in," she said, "for their noon feed." She had a scarred face. "Boy, will it be a mad house?" "Do you need any help?" I said eagerly. "Boy," she said, "some of us have been pouring coffee since two o'clock this morning, steady, without no letup." She started to go. She didn't pay any special attention to me as an individual. She didn't seem to be thinking of me, she didn't seem to see me. I watched her go. I felt rebuffed, hurt. Then I saw instantly she didn't see me because she saw only what she was doing. I ran after her.

I found the kitchen organized like a factory. Nobody asks my name. I am given a large butcher's apron. I realize I have never before worked anonymously. At first I feel strange and then I feel good. The forewoman sets me to washing tin cups. There are not enough cups. We have to wash fast and rinse them and set them up quickly for buttermilk and coffee as the line thickens and the men wait. A little shortish man who is a professional dishwasher is supervising. I feel I won't be able to wash tin cups, but when no one pays any attention except to see that there are enough cups I feel better.

The line grows heavy. The men are coming in from the picket line. Each woman has one thing to do. There is no confusion. I soon learn I am not supposed to help pour the buttermilk. I am not supposed to serve sandwiches. I am supposed to wash tin cups. I suddenly look around and realize all these women are from factories. I know they have learned this organization and specialization in the factory. I look at the round shoulders of the woman cutting bread next to me and I feel I know her. The cups are brought back, washed and put on the counter again. The sweat pours down our faces, but you forget about it.

Then I am changed and put to pouring coffee. At first I look at the men's faces and then I don't look any more. It seems I am pouring coffee for the same tense dirty sweating face, the same body, the same blue shirt and overalls. Hours go by, the heat is terrific. I am not tired. I am hot. I am pouring coffee. I am swung into the most intense and natural organization I have ever felt. I know everything that is going on. These things become of great matter to me.

Eyes looking, hands raising a thousand cups, throats burning, eyes bloodshot from lack of sleep, the body dilated to catch every sound over the whole city. Buttermilk? Coffee?

"Is your man here?" the woman cutting sandwiches asks me.

"No," I say, then I lie for some reason, peering around as if looking eagerly for someone, "I don't see him now."

But I was pouring coffee for living men.

For a long time, about one o'clock, it seemed like something was about to happen. Women seemed to be pouring into headquarters to be near their men. You could hear only lies over the radio. And lies in the papers. Nobody knew precisely what was happening, but everyone thought something would happen in a few hours. You could feel the men being poured out of the hall onto the picket line. Every few minutes cars left and more drew up and were filled. The voice of the loudspeaker was accelerated, calling for men, calling for picket cars.

I could hear the men talking about the arbitration board, the truce that was supposed to be maintained while the board sat with the Governor. They listened to every word over the loudspeaker. A terrible communal excitement ran through the hall like a fire through a forest. I could hardly breathe. I seemed to have no body at all except the body of this excitement. I felt that what had happened before had not been a real movement, these false words and actions had taken place on the periphery. The real action was about to show the real intention.

We kept on pouring thousands of cups of coffee, feeding thousands of men.

The chef with a woman tattooed on his arm was just dishing the last of the stew. It was about two o'clock. The commissary was about empty. We went into the front hall. It was drained of men. The chairs were empty. The voice of the announcer was excited. "The men are massed at the market," he said. "Something is going to happen." I sat down beside a woman who was holding her hands tightly together, leaning forward listening, her eyes bright and dilated. I had never seen her before. She took my hands. She pulled me towards her. She was crying. "It's awful," she said, "something awful is going to happen. They've taken both my children away from me and now something is going to happen to all those men." I held her hands. She had a green ribbon around her hair.

The action seemed reversed. The cars were coming back. The announcer cried, "This is murder." Cars were coming in. I don't know how we got to the stairs. Everyone seemed to be converging at a menaced point. I saw below the crowd stirring, uncoiling. I saw them taking men out of cars and putting them on the hospital cots, on the floor. At first I felt frightened, the close black area of the barn, the blood, the heavy moment, the sense of myself lost, gone. But I couldn't have turned away now. A woman clung to my hand. I was pressed against the body of another. If you are to understand anything you must understand it in the muscular event, in actions we have not been trained for. Something broke all my surfaces in something that was beyond horror and I was dabbing alcohol on the gaping wounds that buckshot makes, hanging open like crying mouths. Buckshot wounds splay in the body and then swell like a blow. Ness, who died, had thirty-eight slugs in his body, in the chest and in the back.

The picket cars kept coming in. Some men have walked back from the market, holding their own blood in. They move in a great explosion, and the newness of the movement makes it seem like something under ether, moving terrifically towards a culmination.

From all over the city workers are coming. They gather outside in two great half-circles, cut in two to let the ambulances in. A traffic cop is still directing traffic at the corner and the crowd cannot stand to see him. "We'll give you just two seconds to beat it," they tell him. He goes away quickly. A striker takes over the street.

Men, women, and children are massing outside, a living circle close packed for protection. From the tall office building businessmen are looking down on the black swarm thickening, coagulating into what action they cannot tell.

We have living blood on our skirts.

That night at eight o'clock a mass meeting was called of all labor. It was to be in a parking lot two blocks from headquarters. All the women gather at the front of the building with collection cans, ready to march to the meeting. I have not been home. It never occurs to me to leave. The twilight is eerie and the men are saying that the chief of police is going to attack the meeting and raid headquarters. The smell of blood hangs in the hot, still air. Rumors strike at the taut nerves. The dusk looks ghastly with what might be in the next half-hour.

"If you have any children," a woman said to me, "you better not go." I looked at the desperate women's faces, the broken feet, the torn and hanging pelvis, the worn and lovely bodies of women who persist under such desperate labors. I shivered, though it was ninety-six and the sun had been down a good hour.

The parking lot was already full of people when we got there and men swarmed the adjoining roofs. An elegant café stood across the street with water sprinkling from its roof and splendidly dressed men and women stood on the steps as if looking at a show.

The platform was the bullet-riddled truck of the afternoon's fray. We had been told to stand close to this platform, so we did, making the center of a wide massed circle that stretched as far as we could see. We seemed buried like minerals in a mass, packed body to body. I felt again that peculiar heavy silence in which there is the real form of the happening. My eyes burn. I can hardly see. I seem to be standing like an animal in ambush. I have the brightest, most physical feeling with every sense sharpened peculiarly. The movements, the masses that I see and feel I have never known before. I only partly know what I am seeing, feeling, but I feel it is the real body and gesture of a future vitality. I see that there is a bright clot of women drawn close to a bullet-riddled truck. I am one of them, yet I don't feel myself at all. It is curious, I feel most alive and yet for the first time in my life I do not feel myself as separate. I realize then that all my previous feelings have been based on feeling myself separate and distinct from others and now I sense sharply faces, bodies, closeness, and my own fear is not my own alone, nor my hope.

The strikers keep moving up cars. We keep moving back together to let cars pass and form between us and a brick building that flanks the parking lot. They are connecting the loudspeaker, testing it. Yes, they are moving up lots of cars, through the crowd and lining them closely side by side. There must be ten thousand people now, heat rising from them. They are standing silent, watching the platform, watching the cars being brought up. The silence seems terrific like a great form moving of itself. This is real movement issuing from the close reality of mass feeling. This is the first real rhythmic movement I have ever seen. My heart hammers terrifically. My hands are swollen and hot. No one is producing this movement. It is a movement upon which all are moving softly, rhythmically, terribly.

No matter how many times I looked at what was happening I hardly knew what I saw. I looked and I saw time and time again that there were men standing close to us, around us, and then suddenly I knew that there was a living chain of men standing shoulder to shoulder, forming a circle around the group of women. They stood shoulder to shoulder slightly moving like a thick vine from the pressure behind, but standing tightly woven like a living wall, moving gently.

I saw that the cars were now lined one close-fitted to the other with strikers sitting on the roofs and closely packed on the running boards. They could see far over the crowd. "What are they doing that for?" I said. No one answered. The wide dilated eyes of the women were like my own. No one seemed to be answering questions now. They simply spoke, cried out, moved together now.

The last car drove in slowly, the crowd letting them through without command or instruction. "A little closer," someone said. "Be sure they are close." Men sprang up to direct whatever action was needed and then subsided again and no one had noticed who it was. They stepped forward to direct a needed action and then fell anonymously back again.

We all watched carefully the placing of the cars. Sometimes we looked at each other. I didn't understand that look. I felt uneasy. It was as if something escaped me. And then suddenly, on my very body, I knew what they were doing, as if it had been communicated to me from a thousand eyes, a thousand silent throats, as if it had been shouted in the loudest voice.

They were building a barricade.

Two men died from that day's shooting. Men lined up to give one of them a blood transfusion, but he died. Black Friday men called the murderous day. Night and day workers held their children up to see the body of Ness who died. Tuesday, the day of the funeral, one thousand more militia were massed downtown.

It was still over ninety in the shade. I went to the funeral parlors and thousands of men and women were massed there waiting in the terrific sun. One block of women and children were standing two hours waiting. I went over and stood near them. I didn't know whether I could march. I didn't like marching in parades. Besides, I felt they might not want me.

I stood aside not knowing if I would march. I couldn't see how they would ever organize it anyway. No one seemed to be doing much.

At three-forty some command went down the ranks. I said foolishly at the last minute, "I don't belong to the auxiliary—could I march?" Three women drew me in. "We want all to march," they said gently. "Come with us."

The giant mass uncoiled like a serpent and straightened out ahead and to my amazement on a lift of road I could see six blocks of massed men, four abreast, with bare heads, moving straight on and as they moved, uncoiled the mass behind and pulled it after them. I felt myself walking, accelerating my speed with the others as the line stretched, pulled taut, then held its rhythm.

Not a cop was in sight. The cortege moved through the stop-and-go signs, it seemed to lift of its own dramatic rhythm, coming from the intention of every person there. We were moving spontaneously in a movement, natural, hardy, and miraculous.

We passed through six blocks of tenements, through a sea of grim faces, and there was not a sound. There was the curious shuffle of thousands of feet, without drum or bugle, in ominous silence, a march not heavy as the military, but very light, exactly with the heart-beat.

I was marching with a million hands, movements, faces, and my own movement was repeating again and again, making a new movement from these many gestures, the walking, falling back, the open mouth crying, the nostrils stretched apart, the raised hand, the blow falling, and the outstretched hand drawing me in.

I felt my legs straighten. I felt my feet join in that strange shuffle of thousands of bodies moving with direction, of thousands of feet, and my own breath with the gigantic breath. As if an electric charge had passed through me, my hair stood on end, I was marching.

Briefly,
ABOUT THE AUTHOR

Meridel Le Sueur was born in Iowa in 1900 and spent most of her life in the Midwest. Her father was the first Socialist mayor of Minto, N. D.; her mother ran for Senator at age 70. After studying at the Academy of Dramatic Art in New York, the only job she could find was as a stunt artist in Hollywood. Her writing career began in 1928 when the populist and worker groups were re-emerging. While writing stories of the early thirties which gained her a national reputation, she reported on strikes, unemployment frays, breadlines, and the plight of farmers in the Midwest. She was on the staff of the *New Masses* and wrote for *The Daily Worker, The American Mercury, The Partisan Review, The Nation, Scribner's Magazine,* and other journals. Acclaimed as a major writer in the thirties, during the McCarthy years, she was blacklisted as a radical from a family of radicals. Much of Ms. Le Sueur's work was published only in periodicals or remains unpublished. Among her published books are *North Star Country, Crusaders, Corn Village, The Lamp in the Spine.* Today, Meridel Le Sueur continues to write, give poetry readings and speak to women's groups, traveling by Greyhound bus.